JUST DAVID

By Eleanor H. Porter

First published in 1916

This unabridged version has updated grammar and spelling.

Cover illustration by Dan Burr

© 2018 Jenny Phillips

goodandbeautiful.com

Table of Contents

CHAPTER 1

The Mountain Home

F
AR UP ON THE MOUNTAINSIDE, THE LITTLE SHACK STOOD
alone in the clearing. It was roughly yet warmly built.
Behind it jagged cliffs broke the north wind, and towered
gray-white in the sunshine. Before it a tiny expanse of green sloped
gently away to a point where the mountain dropped in another
sharp descent, wooded with scrubby firs and pines. At the left a
footpath led into the cool depths of the forest. But at the right, the
mountain fell away again and disclosed to view the picture David
loved the best of all: the far-reaching valley; the silver pool of the
lake with its ribbon of a river flung far out; and above it the grays
and greens and purples of the mountains that climbed one upon
another's shoulders until the topmost thrust their heads into the
wide dome of the sky itself.

There was no road, apparently, leading away from the cabin.
There was only the footpath that disappeared into the forest.
Neither, anywhere, was there a house in sight nearer than the
white specks far down in the valley by the river.

Within the shack a wide fireplace dominated one side of
the main room. It was June now, and the ashes lay cold on the
hearth; but from the tiny lean-to in the rear came the smell and
the sputter of bacon sizzling over a blaze. The furnishings of the
room were simple, yet in a way, out of the common. There were
two bunks, a few rude but comfortable chairs, a table, two music-

racks, two violins with their cases, and everywhere books and scattered sheets of music. Nowhere was there cushion, curtain, or knickknack that told of a woman's taste or touch. On the other hand, neither was there anywhere gun, pelt, or antlered head that spoke of a man's strength and skill. For decoration there was a beautiful copy of the Sistine Madonna, several photographs signed with names well known out in the great world beyond the mountains, and a festoon of pine cones such as a child might gather and hang.

From the little lean-to kitchen the sound of the sputtering suddenly ceased, and at the door appeared a pair of dark, wistful eyes.

"Daddy!" called the owner of the eyes.

There was no answer.

"Father, are you there?" called the voice, more insistently.

From one of the bunks came a slight stir and a murmured word. At the sound the boy at the door leaped softly into the room and hurried to the bunk in the corner. He was a slender lad with short, crisp curls at his ears, and the red of perfect health in his cheeks. His hands, slim and long, reached forward eagerly.

"Daddy, come! I've done the bacon all myself, and the potatoes and the coffee, too. Quick, it's all getting cold!"

Slowly, with the aid of the boy's firm hands, the man pulled himself half to a sitting posture. His cheeks, like the boy's, were red—but not with health. His eyes were a little wild, but his voice was low and very tender, like a caress.

"David—it's my little son David!"

"Of course it's David! Who else should it be?" laughed the boy. "Come!" And he tugged at the man's hands.

The man rose then, unsteadily, and by sheer will forced himself to stand upright. The wild look left his eyes, and the flush his cheeks. His face looked suddenly old and haggard. Yet, with fairly sure steps he crossed the room and entered the little kitchen.

Half of the bacon was black; the other half was transparent and like tough jelly. The potatoes were soggy and had the unmistakable taste that comes from a dish that has boiled dry. The coffee was lukewarm and muddy. Even the milk was sour.

David laughed a little ruefully.

"Things aren't so nice as yours, Father," he apologized. "I'm afraid I'm nothing but a discord in that orchestra today! Somehow, some of the stove was hotter than the rest, and burnt up the bacon in spots; and all the water got out of the potatoes, too—though *that* didn't matter, for I just put more cold in. I forgot and left the milk in the sun, and it tastes bad now; but I'm sure next time it'll be better—all of it."

The man smiled, but he shook his head sadly.

"But there ought not to be any 'next time,' David."

"Why not? What do you mean? Aren't you ever going to let me try again, Father?" There was real distress in the boy's voice.

The man hesitated. His lips parted with an indrawn breath, as if behind them lay a rush of words. But they closed abruptly, the words still unsaid. Then, very lightly, came these others:

"Well, son, this isn't a very nice way to treat your supper, is it? Now, if you please, I'll take some of that bacon. I think I feel my appetite coming back."

If the truant appetite "came back," however, it could not have stayed; for the man ate but little. He frowned, too, as he saw how little the boy ate. He sat silent while his son cleared the food and dishes away, and he was still silent when, with the boy, he passed out of the house and walked to the little bench facing the west.

Unless it stormed very hard, David never went to bed without this last look at his "Silver Lake," as he called the little sheet of water far down in the valley.

"Daddy, it's gold tonight—all gold with the sun!" he cried

rapturously, as his eyes fell upon his treasure. "Oh, daddy!"

It was a long-drawn cry of ecstasy, and hearing it, the man winced, as with sudden pain.

"Daddy, I'm going to play it—I've got to play it!" cried the boy, bounding toward the cabin. In a moment he had returned, violin at his chin.

The man watched and listened; and as he watched and listened, his face became a battle-ground whereon pride and fear, hope and despair, joy and sorrow fought for the mastery.

It was no new thing for David to "play" the sunset. Always, when he was moved, David turned to his violin. Always in its quivering strings he found the means to say that which his tongue could not express.

Across the valley the grays and blues of the mountains had become all purples now. Above, the sky in one vast flame of crimson and gold, was a molten sea on which floated rose-pink cloud-boats. Below, the valley with its lake and river picked out in rose and gold against the shadowy greens of field and forest, seemed like some land of loveliness.

And all this was in David's violin, and all this, too, was on David's uplifted, rapturous face.

As the last rose-glow turned to gray and the last strain quivered into silence, the man spoke. His voice was almost harsh with self-control.

"David, the time has come. We'll have to give it up—you and I."

The boy turned wonderingly, his face still softly luminous.

"Give what up?"

"This—all this."

"This! Why, Father, what do you mean? This is home!"

The man nodded wearily.

"I know. It has been home; but, David, you didn't think we could always live here, like this, did you?"

David laughed softly, and turned his eyes once more to the distant sky-line.

"Why not?" he asked dreamily. "What better place could there be? I like it, Daddy."

The man drew a troubled breath, and stirred restlessly. The teasing pain in his side was very bad tonight, and no change of position eased it. He was ill, very ill; and he knew it. Yet he also knew that, to David, sickness, pain, and death meant nothing—or, at most, words that had always been lightly, almost unconsciously passed over. For the first time he wondered if, after all, his training—some of it—had been wise.

For six years he had had the boy under his exclusive care and guidance. For six years the boy had eaten the food, worn the clothing, and studied the books of his father's choosing. For six years that father had thought, planned, breathed, moved, lived for his son. There had been no others in the little cabin. There had been only the occasional trips through the woods to the little town on the mountainside for food and clothing to break the days of close companionship.

All this the man had planned carefully. He had meant that only the good and beautiful should have place in David's youth. It was not that he intended that evil, unhappiness, and death should lack definition, only definiteness, in the boy's mind. It should be a case where the good and the beautiful should so fill the thoughts that there would be no room for anything else. This had been his plan. And thus far he had succeeded—succeeded so wonderfully that he began now, in the face of his own illness, and of what he feared would come of it, to doubt the wisdom of that planning.

As he looked at the boy's rapt face, he remembered David's surprised questioning at the first dead squirrel he had found in the woods. David was six then.

"Why, Daddy, he's asleep, and he won't wake up!" he had cried.

Then, after a gentle touch: "And he's cold—oh, so cold!"

The father had hurried his son away at the time, and had evaded his questions; and David had seemed content. But the next day the boy had gone back to the subject. His eyes were wide then, and a little frightened.

"Father, what is it to be—dead?"

"What do you mean, David?"

"The boy who brings the milk—he had the squirrel this morning. He said it was not asleep. It was—dead."

"It means that the squirrel, the real squirrel under the fur, has gone away, David."

"Where?"

"To a far country, perhaps."

"Will he come back?"

"No."

"Did he want to go?"

"We'll hope so."

"But he left his—his fur coat behind him. Didn't he need—that?"

"No, or he'd have taken it with him."

David had fallen silent at this. He had remained strangely silent indeed for some days; then, out in the woods with his father one morning, he gave a joyous shout. He was standing by the ice-covered brook, and looking at a little black hole through which the hurrying water could be plainly seen.

"Daddy, oh, Daddy, I know now how it is, about being—dead."

"Why—David!"

"It's like the water in the brook, you know; *that's* going to a far country, and it isn't coming back. And it leaves its little cold ice-coat behind it just as the squirrel did, too. It doesn't need it. It can go without it. Don't you see? And it's singing—listen!—it's singing as it goes. It *wants* to go!"

"Yes, David." And David's father had sighed with relief that his son had found his own explanation of the mystery, and one that satisfied.

Later, in his books, David found death again. It was a man, this time. The boy had looked up with startled eyes.

"Do people, real people, like you and me, be dead, Father? Do they go to a far country?

"Yes, son, in time—to a far country ruled over by a great and good King they tell us."

David's father had trembled as he said it, and had waited fearfully for the result. But David had only smiled happily as he answered:

"But they go singing, Father, like the little brook. You know I heard it!"

And there the matter had ended. David was ten now, and not yet for him did death spell terror. Because of this David's father was relieved; and yet—still because of this—he was afraid.

"David," he said gently. "Listen to me."

The boy turned with a long sigh.

"Yes, Father."

"We must go away. Out in the great world there are men and women and children waiting for you. You've a beautiful work to do; and one can't do one's work on a mountain-top."

"Why not? I like it here, and I've always been here."

"Not always, David; six years. You were four when I brought you here. You don't remember, perhaps."

David shook his head. His eyes were again dreamily fixed on the sky.

"I think I'd like it—to go—if I could sail away on that little cloud-boat up there," he murmured.

The man sighed and shook his head.

"We can't go on cloud-boats. We must walk, David, for a way—

and we must go soon—soon," he added feverishly. "I must get you back—back among friends, before—"

He rose unsteadily, and tried to walk erect. His limbs shook, and the blood throbbed at his temples. He was appalled at his weakness. With a fierceness born of his terror he turned sharply to the boy at his side.

"David, we've got to go! We've got to go—Tomorrow!"

"Father!"

"Yes, yes, come!" He stumbled blindly, yet in some way he reached the cabin door.

Behind him David still sat, inert, staring. The next minute the boy had sprung to his feet and was hurrying after his father.

CHAPTER 2

The Trail

A CURIOUS STRENGTH SEEMED TO HAVE COME TO THE MAN. With almost steady hands he took down the photographs and the Sistine Madonna, packing them neatly away in a box to be left. From beneath his bunk he dragged a large, dusty traveling bag, and in this he stowed a little food, a few garments, and a great deal of the music scattered about the room.

David, in the doorway, stared in dazed wonder. Gradually, into his eyes crept a look never seen there before.

"Father, where are we going?" he asked at last in a shaking voice, as he came slowly into the room.

"Back, son; we're going back."

"To the village, where we get our eggs and bacon?"

"No, no, lad, not there. The other way. We go down into the valley this time."

"The valley—MY valley, with the Silver Lake?"

"Yes, my son—and beyond—far beyond." The man spoke dreamily. He was looking at a photograph in his hand. It had slipped in among the loose sheets of music and had not been put away with the others. It was the likeness of a beautiful woman.

For a moment David eyed him uncertainly; then he spoke.

"Daddy, who is that? Who are all these people in the pictures? You've never told me about any of them except the little round one that you wear in your pocket. Who are they?"

Instead of answering, the man turned faraway eyes on the boy and smiled wistfully.

"Ah, David, lad, how they'll love you! How they will love you! But you mustn't let them spoil you, son. You must remember— remember all I've told you."

Once again David asked his question, but this time the man only turned back to the photograph, muttering something the boy could not understand.

After that David did not question any more. He was too amazed, too distressed. He had never before seen his father like this. With nervous haste the man was setting the little room to rights, crowding things into the bag, and packing other things away in an old trunk. His cheeks were very red, and his eyes very bright. He talked, too, almost constantly, though David could understand scarcely a word of what was said. Later, the man caught up his violin and played; and never before had David heard his father play like that. The boy's eyes filled, and his heart ached with a pain that choked and numbed—though why, David could not have told. Still later, the man dropped his violin and sank exhausted into a chair; and then David, worn and frightened with it all, crept to his bunk and fell asleep.

In the gray dawn of the morning David awoke to a different world. His father, white-faced and gentle, was calling him to get ready for breakfast. The little room, dismantled of its decorations, was bare and cold. The bag, closed and strapped, rested on the floor by the door, together with the two violins in their cases, ready to carry.

"We must hurry, son. It's a long tramp before we take the cars."

"The cars—the real cars? Do we go in those?" David was fully awake now.

"Yes."

"And is that all we're to carry?"

"Yes. Hurry, son."

"But we will come back—sometime?"

There was no answer.

"Father, we're coming back—sometime?" David's voice was insistent now.

The man stooped and tightened a strap that was already quite tight enough. Then he laughed lightly.

"Why, of course you're coming back sometime, David. Only think of all these things we're leaving!"

When the last dish was put away, the last garment adjusted, and the last look given to the little room, the travelers picked up the bag and the violins, and went out into the sweet freshness of the morning. As he fastened the door, the man sighed profoundly; but David did not notice this. His face was turned toward the east—always, David looked toward the sun.

"Daddy, let's not go, after all! Let's stay here," he cried ardently, drinking in the beauty of the morning.

"We must go, David. Come, son." And the man led the way across the green slope to the west.

It was a scarcely perceptible trail, but the man found it, and followed it with evident confidence. There was only the pause now and then to steady his none-too-sure step, or to ease the burden of the bag. Very soon, the forest lay all about them, with the birds singing over their heads, and with numberless tiny feet scurrying through the underbrush on all sides. Just out of sight, a brook babbled noisily of its delight in being alive; and away up in the treetops the morning sun played hide-and-seek among the dancing leaves.

And David leaped, and laughed, and loved it all, nor was any of it strange to him. The birds, the trees, the sun, the brook, the scurrying little creatures of the forest, all were friends of his. But the man—the man did not leap or laugh, though he, too, loved it all. The man was afraid.

He knew now that he had undertaken more than he could carry out. Step by step the bag had grown heavier, and hour by hour the insistent, teasing pain in his side had increased until now it was a torture. He had forgotten that the way to the valley was so long; he had not realized how nearly spent was his strength before he even started down the trail. Throbbing through his brain was the question, what if, after all, he could not—but even to himself he would not say the words.

At noon they paused for luncheon, and at night they camped where the chattering brook had stopped to rest in a still, black pool. The next morning, the man and the boy picked up the trail again, but without the bag. Under some leaves in a little hollow, the man had hidden the bag, and had then said, as if casually—

"I believe, after all, I won't carry this along. There's nothing in it that we really need, you know, now that I've taken out the luncheon box, and by night we'll be down in the valley."

"Of course!" laughed David. "We don't need that." And he laughed again, for pure joy. Little use had David for bags or baggage!

They were more than halfway down the mountain now, and soon they reached a grass-grown road, little traveled, but yet a road. Still later, they came to where four ways crossed, and two of them bore the marks of many wheels. By sundown, the little brook at their side murmured softly of quiet fields and meadows, and David knew that the valley was reached.

David was not laughing now. He was watching his father with startled eyes. David had not known what anxiety was. He was finding out now—though he but vaguely realized that something was not right. For some time his father had said but little, and that little had been in a voice that was thick and unnatural-sounding. He was walking fast, yet David noticed that every step seemed an effort, and that every breath came in short gasps. His eyes were very bright and were fixedly bent on the road ahead, as if even the haste he was making was not haste enough. Twice David spoke to him, but he did not answer; and the boy could only trudge along on his weary little feet and sigh for the dear home on the mountain-top which they had left behind them the morning before.

They met few fellow travelers, and those they did meet paid scant attention to the man and the boy carrying the violins. As it chanced, there was no one in sight when the man, walking in the grass at the side of the road, stumbled and fell heavily to the ground.

David sprang quickly forward.

"Father, what is it? *What is it?*"

There was no answer.

"Daddy, why don't you speak to me? See, it's David!"

With a painful effort the man roused himself and sat up. For a moment he gazed dully into the boy's face; then a half-forgotten something seemed to stir him into feverish action. With shaking fingers he handed David his watch and a small ivory miniature. Then he searched his pockets until on the ground before him lay a shining pile of gold pieces—to David there seemed to be a hundred of them.

"Take them—hide them—keep them. David, until you—need them," panted the man. "Then go—go on. I can't."

"Alone? Without you?" demurred the boy, aghast. "Why, father, I couldn't! I don't know the way. Besides, I'd rather stay with you," he added soothingly, as he slipped the watch and the miniature into his pocket; "then we can both go." And he dropped himself down at his father's side.

The man shook his head feebly, and pointed again to the gold pieces.

"Take them, David—hide them," he chattered with pale lips.

Almost impatiently the boy began picking up the money and tucking it into his pockets.

"But, Father, I'm not going without you," he declared stoutly, as the last bit of gold slipped out of sight and a horse and wagon rattled around the turn of the road above.

The driver of the horse glanced disapprovingly at the man and the boy by the roadside, but he did not stop. After he had passed, the boy turned again to his father. The man was fumbling once more in his pockets. This time from his coat he produced a pencil and a small notebook from which he tore a page and began to write, laboriously, painfully.

David sighed and looked about him. He was tired and hungry, and he did not understand things at all. Something very wrong, very terrible, must be the matter with his father. Here it was almost dark, yet they had no place to go, no supper to eat, while far, far up on the mountainside was their own dear home sad and lonely without them. Up there, too, the sun still shone, doubtless—at least there were the rose-glow and Silver Lake to look at, while down here there was nothing, nothing but gray shadows, a long dreary road, and a straggling house or two in sight. From above, the valley might look to be a land of loveliness, but in reality it was nothing but a dismal waste of gloom, decided David.

David's father had torn a second page from his book and was beginning another note, when the boy suddenly jumped to his feet. One of the straggling houses was near the road where they sat, and its presence had given David an idea. With swift steps he hurried to the front door and knocked upon it. In answer a tall, unsmiling woman appeared, and said, "Well?"

David removed his cap as his father had taught him to do when one of the mountain women spoke to him.

"Good evening, lady; I'm David," he began frankly. "My father is so tired he fell down back there, and we should like very much to stay with you all night, if you don't mind."

The woman in the doorway stared. For a moment she was

dumb with amazement. Her eyes swept the plain, rather rough garments of the boy, then sought the half-recumbent figure of the man by the roadside. Her chin came up angrily.

"Oh, would you, indeed! Well, upon my word!" she shouted. "Humph! We don't accommodate tramps, little boy." And she shut the door hard.

It was David's turn to stare. Just what a tramp might be, he did not know, but never before had a request of his been so angrily refused. He knew that. A fierce something rose within him—a fierce new something that sent the swift red to his neck and brow. He raised a determined hand to the doorknob—he had something to say to that woman—when the door suddenly opened again from the inside.

"See here, boy," began the woman, looking out at him a little less unkindly, "if you're hungry I'll give you some milk and bread. Go around to the back porch, and I'll get it for you." And she shut the door again.

David's hand dropped to his side. The red still stayed on his face and neck, however, and that fierce new something within him bade him refuse to take food from this woman . . . But there was his father—his poor father, who was so tired; and there was his own stomach clamoring to be fed. No, he could not refuse. And with slow steps and hanging head David went around the corner of the house to the rear.

As the half loaf of bread and the pail of milk were placed in his hands, David remembered suddenly that in the village store on the mountain, his father paid money for his food. David was glad, now, that he had those gold pieces in his pocket, for he could pay money. Instantly his head came up. Once more erect with self respect, he shifted his burdens to one hand and thrust the other into his pocket. A moment later he presented on his outstretched palm a shining disk of gold.

"Will you take this, to pay, please, for the bread and milk?" he asked proudly.

The woman began to shake her head, but, as her eyes fell on the money, she started, and bent closer to examine it. The next instant she jerked herself upright with an angry exclamation.

"It's gold! A ten dollar gold piece! So you're a thief, too, are you, as well as a tramp? Humph! Well, I guess you don't need this then," she finished sharply, snatching the bread and the pail of milk from the boy's hand.

The next moment, David stood alone on the doorstep, with the sound of a quickly thrown bolt in his ears.

A thief! David knew little of thieves, but he knew what they were. Only a month before, a man had tried to steal the violins from the cabin, and he was a thief, the milk boy said. David flushed now again, angrily, as he faced the closed door. But he did not tarry. He turned and ran to his father.

"Father, come away, quick! You must come away," he choked.

So urgent was the boy's voice that almost unconsciously the sick man got to his feet. With shaking hands he thrust the notes he had been writing into his pocket. The little book, from which he had torn the leaves for this purpose, had already dropped unheeded into the grass at his feet.

"Yes, son, yes, we'll go," muttered the man. "I feel better now. I can—walk."

And he did walk, though very slowly, ten, a dozen, twenty steps. From behind came the sound of wheels that stopped close beside them.

"Hullo, there! Going to the village?" called a voice.

"Yes, sir." David's answer was unhesitating. Where "the village" was, he did not know. He knew only that it must be somewhere away from the woman who had called him a thief. And that was all he cared to know.

"I'm going 'most there myself. Want a lift?" asked the man, still kindly.

"Yes, sir. Thank you!" cried the boy joyfully. And together they aided his father to climb into the roomy wagon-body.

There were few words said. The man at the reins drove rapidly, and paid little attention to anything but his horses. The sick man dozed and rested. The boy sat, wistful-eyed and silent, watching the trees and houses flit by. The sun had long ago set, but it was not dark, for the moon was round and bright, and the sky was cloudless. Where the road forked sharply the man drew his horses to a stop.

"Well, I'm sorry, but I guess I'll have to drop you here, friends. I turn off to the right; but 't ain't more 'n a quarter of a mile for you, now," he finished cheerily, pointing with his whip to a cluster of twinkling lights.

"Thank you, sir, thank you," breathed David gratefully, steadying his father's steps. "You've helped us lots. Thank you!"

In David's heart was a wild desire to lay at his good man's feet all of his shining gold pieces as payment for this timely aid. But caution held him back: it seemed that only in stores did money pay; outside it branded one as a thief!

Alone with his father, David faced once more his problem. Where should they go for the night? Plainly his father could not walk far. He had begun to talk again, too—low, half-finished sentences that David could not understand, and that vaguely troubled him. There was a house near by, and several others down the road toward the village, but David had had all the experience he wanted that night with strange houses and strange women. There was a barn, a big one, which was nearest of all, and it was toward this barn that David finally turned his father's steps.

"We'll go there, daddy, if we can get in," he proposed softly. "And we'll stay all night and rest."

CHAPTER 3

The Valley

THE LONG TWILIGHT OF THE JUNE DAY HAD CHANGED into a night that was scarcely darker, so bright was the moonlight. Seen from the house, the barn and the low buildings beyond loomed shadowy and unreal, yet very beautiful. On the side porch of the house sat Simeon Holly and his wife, content to rest mind and body only because a full day's work lay well done behind them.

It was just as Simeon rose to his feet to go indoors that a long note from a violin reached their ears.

"Simeon!" cried the woman. "What was that?"

The man did not answer. His eyes were fixed on the barn.

"Simeon, it's a fiddle!" exclaimed Mrs. Holly, as a second tone quivered on the air. "And it's in our barn!"

Simeon's jaw set. With a stern word, he crossed the porch and entered the kitchen. In another minute he had returned, a lighted lantern in his hand.

"Simeon, d-don't go," begged the woman, tremulously. "You—you don't know what's there."

"Fiddles are not played without hands, Ellen," retorted the man severely. "Would you have me go to bed and leave a half-drunken, ungodly minstrel fellow in possession of our barn? Tonight, on my way home, I passed a pretty pair of them lying by the roadside—a man and a boy with two violins. They're the culprits, likely—

though how they got this far, I don't see. Do you think I want to leave my barn to tramps like them?"

"N-no, I suppose not," faltered the woman as she rose tremblingly to her feet and followed her husband's shadow across the yard.

Once inside the barn, Simeon Holly and his wife paused involuntarily. The music was all about them now, filling the air with runs and trills and rollicking bits of melody. Giving an angry exclamation, the man turned then to the narrow stairway and climbed to the hayloft above. At his heels came his wife, and so her eyes, almost as soon as his, fell upon the man lying back on the hay with the moonlight full upon his face. Instantly, the music dropped to a whisper, and a low voice came out of the gloom beyond the square of moonlight which came from the window in the roof.

"If you'll please be as still as you can, sir. You see, he's asleep and he's so tired," said the voice.

For a moment the man and the woman on the stairway paused in amazement, then the man lifted his lantern and strode toward the voice.

"Who are you? What are you doing here?" he demanded sharply.

A boy's face, round, tanned, and just now a bit anxious, flashed out of the dark. "Oh, please, sir, if you would speak lower," pleaded the boy. "He's so tired! I'm David, sir, and that's my father. We came in here to rest and sleep."

Simeon Holly's unrelenting gaze left the boy's face and swept that of the man lying back on the hay. The next instant, he lowered the lantern and leaned nearer, putting forth a cautious hand. At once he straightened himself, muttering a brusque word under his breath. Then he turned with the angry question, "Boy, what do you mean by playing a jig on your fiddle at such a time as this?"

"Why, Father asked me to play," returned the boy cheerily. "He said he could walk through green forests then, with the ripple of brooks in his ears, and that the birds and the squirrels—"

"See here, boy, who are you?" cut in Simeon Holly sternly. "Where did you come from?"

"From home, sir."

"Where is that?"

"Why, home, sir, where I live. In the mountains, 'way up, up, up—oh, so far up! And there's such a big, big sky, so much nicer than down here." The boy's voice quivered and almost broke, and his eyes constantly sought the white face on the hay.

It was then that Simeon Holly awoke to the sudden realization that it was time for action. He turned to his wife.

"Take the boy to the house," he directed incisively. "We'll have to keep him tonight, I suppose. I'll go for Higgins. Of course, the whole thing will have to be put in his hands at once. You can't do anything here," he added, as he caught her questioning glance. "Leave everything just as it is. The man is dead."

"Dead?" It was a sharp cry from the boy, yet there was more of wonder than of terror in it. "Do you mean that he has gone—like the water in the brook—to the far country?" he faltered.

Simeon Holly stared. Then he said more distinctly, "Your father is dead, boy."

"And he won't come back any more?" David's voice broke now.

There was no answer. Mrs. Holly caught her breath convulsively and looked away. Even Simeon Holly refused to meet the boy's pleading eyes.

With a quick cry David sprang to his father's side. "But he's here—right here," he challenged shrilly. "Daddy, Daddy, speak to me! It's David!" Reaching out his hand, he gently touched his father's face. He drew back then, at once, his eyes distended with terror. "He isn't! He is—gone," he chattered frenziedly. "This isn't the father-part that knows. It's the other—that they leave. He's left it behind him—like the squirrel, and the water in the brook."

Suddenly the boy's face changed. It grew rapt and luminous as he leaped to his feet, crying joyously: "But he asked me to play, so he went singing—singing, just as he said that they did. And I made him walk through green forests with the ripple of the brooks in his ears! Listen—like this!" And once more the boy raised the violin to his chin, and once more the music trilled and rippled about the shocked, amazed ears of Simeon Holly and his wife.

For a time neither the man nor the woman could speak. There was nothing in their humdrum, habit-smoothed tilling of the soil and washing of pots and pans to prepare them for a scene like this—a moonlit barn, a strange dead man, and that dead man's son babbling of brooks and squirrels and playing jigs on a fiddle for a dirge. At last, however, Simeon found his voice.

"Boy, boy, stop that!" he thundered. "Are you mad—clean mad? Go into the house, I say!" And the boy, dazed but obedient, put up his violin and followed the woman, who, with tear-blinded eyes, was leading the way down the stairs.

Mrs. Holly was frightened, but she was also strangely moved. From the long ago the sound of another violin had come to her—a violin, too, played by a boy's hands. But of this, all this, Mrs. Holly did not like to think.

In the kitchen now, she turned and faced her young guest.

"Are you hungry, little boy?"

David hesitated; he had not forgotten the woman, the milk, and the gold piece.

"Are you hungry—dear?" stammered Mrs. Holly again; and this time David's clamorous stomach forced a "yes" from his unwilling lips, which sent Mrs. Holly at once into the pantry for bread and milk and a heaped-up plate of doughnuts such as David had never seen before.

David ate his supper like any hungry boy might; and Mrs. Holly, in the face of this very ordinary sight of hunger being appeased at her table, breathed more freely and ventured to think that perhaps this strange little boy was not so very strange, after all.

"What is your name?" she found courage to ask then.

"David."

"David what?"

"Just David."

"But your father's name?" Mrs. Holly had almost asked, but stopped in time. She did not want to speak of him. "Where do you live?" she asked instead.

"On the mountain, way up, up on the mountain where I can see my Silver Lake every day, you know."

"But you didn't live there alone?"

"Oh, no, with father—before he—went away," faltered the boy. The woman flushed red and bit her lip.

"No, no, I mean, were there no other houses but yours?" she stammered.

"No, ma'am."

"But, wasn't your mother anywhere?"

"Oh, yes, in Father's pocket."

"Your mother—in your father's pocket!"

So plainly aghast was the questioner that David looked not a little surprised as he explained, "You don't understand. She is an angel-mother, and angel-mothers don't have anything, only their pictures, down here with us. And that's what we have, and Father always carried it in his pocket."

"Oh—" murmured Mrs. Holly, a quick mist in her eyes. Then gently, "And did you always live there, on the mountain?"

"Six years, Father said."

"But what did you do all day? Weren't you ever—lonesome?"

"Lonesome?" The boy's eyes were puzzled.

"Yes. Didn't you miss things—people, other houses, boys of your own age, and—and such things?"

David's eyes widened. "Why, how could I?" he cried. "When I had Daddy, and my violin, and my Silver Lake, and the whole of the great big woods with everything in them to talk to, and to talk to me?"

"Woods, and things in them to—to talk to you!"

"Why, yes. It was the little brook, you know, after the squirrel, that told me about being dead, and—"

"Yes, yes, but never mind now, dear," stammered the woman, rising hurriedly to her feet. The boy was a little wild, after all, she thought. "You—you should go to bed. Haven't you a—a bag, or—or anything?"

"No, ma'am, we left it," smiled David apologetically. "You see, we had so much in it that it got too heavy to carry. So we didn't bring it."

"So much in it you didn't bring it, indeed!" repeated Mrs. Holly under her breath, throwing up her hands with a gesture of despair. "Boy, what are you, anyway?"

It was not meant for a question, but to the woman's surprise, the boy answered, frankly, simply, "Father says that I'm one little instrument in the great Orchestra of Life, and that I must see to it that I'm always in tune, and don't drag or hit false notes."

"My land!" breathed the woman, dropping back in her chair, her eyes fixed on the boy. Then, with an effort, she got to her feet.

"Come, you must go to bed," she stammered. "I'm sure bed is—is the best place for you. I think I can find what—what you need," she finished feebly.

Some minutes later, in a snug little room over the kitchen, David found himself alone at last. The room, though it had once belonged to a boy of his own age, looked very strange to David.

On the floor was a rag carpet rug, the first he had ever seen. On the walls were a fishing rod, a toy shotgun, and a case full of bugs and moths, each little body impaled on a pin, to David's shuddering horror. The bed had four tall posts at the corners and a very puffy top that filled David with wonder as to how he was to reach it, or stay there if he did gain it. Across a chair lay a boy's long yellow-white nightshirt that the kind lady had left, after hurriedly wiping her eyes with the edge of its hem. In all the circle of the candlelight, there was just one familiar object to David's homesick eyes—the long black violin case which he had brought in himself, and which held his beloved violin.

With his back carefully turned toward the impaled bugs and moths on the wall, David undressed himself and slipped into the yellow-white nightshirt, which he sniffed at gratefully, so like pine woods was the perfume that hung about its folds. Then he blew out the candle and groped his way to the one window the little room contained.

The moon still shone, but little could be seen through the thick green branches of the tree outside. From the yard below came the sound of wheels and of men's excited voices. There came also the twinkle of lanterns borne by hurrying hands and the tramp of shuffling feet. In the window, David shivered. There were no wide sweep of mountain, hill, and valley, no Silver Lake, no restful hush, no Daddy—no beautiful Things that Were. There was only the dreary, hollow mockery of the Things they had Become.

Long minutes later, David, with the violin in his arms, lay down upon the rug, and for the first time since babyhood, he sobbed himself to sleep—but it was a sleep that brought no rest, for in it he dreamed that he was a big, white-winged moth pinned with a star to an ink-black sky.

CHAPTER 4

Two Letters

IN THE EARLY GRAY DAWN DAVID AWOKE. HIS FIRST SENSATION was the physical numbness and stiffness that came from his hard bed on the floor.

"Why, Daddy," he began, pulling himself half erect, "I slept all night on—" He stopped suddenly, brushing his eyes with the backs of his hands. "Why, Daddy, where—" Then full consciousness came to him.

With a low cry, he sprang to his feet and ran to the window. Through the trees he could see the sunrise glow of the eastern sky. Down in the yard, no one was in sight, but the barn door was open, and with a quick in-drawing of his breath, David turned back into the room and began to thrust himself into his clothing.

The gold in his sagging pockets clinked and jingled musically; and once, half a dozen pieces rolled out upon the floor. For a moment the boy looked as if he was going to let them remain where they were. But the next minute, with an impatient gesture, he had picked them up and thrust them deep into one of his pockets, silencing their jingling with his handkerchief.

Once dressed, David picked up his violin and stepped softly into the hall. At first, no sound reached his ears. Then, from the kitchen below came the clatter of brisk feet and the rattle of tins and crockery. Tightening his clasp on the violin, David slipped quietly down the back stairs and out to the yard. It was only a few seconds then before he was hurrying through the open doorway of the barn and up the narrow stairway to the loft above.

At the top, however, he came to a sharp pause, with a low cry. The next moment he turned to see a kindly-faced man looking up at him from the foot of the stairs.

"Oh, sir, please—please, where is he? What have you done with him?" appealed the boy, almost plunging headlong down the stairs in his haste to reach the bottom.

Into the man's weather-beaten face came a look of sincere but awkward sympathy. "Oh, hello, Sonny! So you're the boy, are ye?" he began diffidently.

"Yes, yes, I'm David. But where is he—my father, you know? I mean the—the part he—he left behind him?" choked the boy. "The part like—the ice-coat?"

The man stared. Then, involuntarily, he began to back away. "Well, ye see, I— I—"

"But maybe you don't know," interrupted David feverishly. "You aren't the man I saw last night. Who are you? Where is he—the other one, please?"

"No, I— I wasn't here. That is, not at the first," spoke up the man quickly, still unconsciously backing away. "Me, I'm only Larson, Perry Larson, ye know. It was Mr. Holly you see last night—him that I works for."

"Then where is Mr. Holly, please?" faltered the boy, hurrying toward the barn door. "Maybe he would know—about Father. Oh, there he is!" And David ran out of the barn and across the yard to the kitchen porch.

It was an unhappy ten minutes that David spent then. Besides Mr. Holly, there were Mrs. Holly and the man, Perry Larson. And they all talked. But little of what they said could David understand. To none of his questions could he obtain an answer that satisfied.

Neither, on his part, could he seem to reply to their questions in a way that pleased them.

They went in to breakfast then, Mr. and Mrs. Holly, and the man, Perry Larson. They asked David to go—at least, Mrs. Holly asked him. But David shook his head and said, "No, no, thank you very much. I'd rather not, if you please—not now." Then he dropped himself down on the steps to think. As if he could eat—with that great choking lump in his throat that refused to be swallowed!

David was thoroughly dazed, frightened, and dismayed. He knew now that never again in this world would he see his dear father, or hear him speak. This much had been made very clear to him during the last ten minutes. Why this should be so, or what his father would want him to do, he could not seem to find out. Not until now had he realized at all what this going away of his father was to mean to him. And he told himself frantically that he could not have it so. *He could not have it so*! But even as he said the words, he knew that it was so—diffidently so.

David began then to long for his mountain home. There, at least, he would have his dear forest all about him, with the birds and the squirrels and the friendly little brooks. There he would have his Silver Lake to look at, too, and all of them would speak to him of his father. He believed, indeed, that up there, it would almost seem as if his father were really with him. And, anyway, if his father ever should come back, it would be there that he would be sure to seek him—up there in the little mountain home so dear to them both. Back to the cabin he would go now, then. Yes, indeed he would!

With a low word and a passionately intent expression, David got to his feet, picked up his violin, and hurried, firm-footed, down the driveway and out upon the main highway, turning in the direction from whence he had come with his father the night before.

The Hollys had just finished breakfast when Higgins, the coroner, drove into the yard accompanied by William Streeter, the town's most prominent farmer—and the most miserly one, if report was to be credited.

"Well, could you get anything out of the boy?" demanded Higgins, without ceremony, as Simeon Holly and Larson appeared on the kitchen porch.

"Very little. Really nothing of importance," answered Simeon Holly.

"Where is he now?"

"Why, he was here on the steps a few minutes ago." Simeon Holly looked about him a bit impatiently.

"Well, I want to see him. I've got a letter for him."

"A letter!" exclaimed Simeon Holly and Larson in amazed unison.

"Yes. Found it in his father's pocket," nodded the coroner, with all the tantalizing brevity of a man who knows he has a choice morsel of information that is eagerly awaited. "It's addressed to 'My boy David,' so I calculated we'd better give it to him first without reading it, seeing it's his. After he reads it, though, I want to see it. I want to see if what it says is any nearer being horse-sense than the other one is."

"The other one!" exclaimed the amazed chorus again.

"Oh, yes, there's another one," spoke up William Streeter tersely. "And I've read it—all but the scrawl at the end. There couldn't anybody read that!" Higgins laughed.

"Well, I'm free to confess it is a sticker—that name," he admitted. "And it's the name we want, of course, to tell us who they are—since it seems the boy don't know, from what you said last night. I was in hopes, by this morning, you'd have found out more from him."

Simeon Holly shook his head.

"It was impossible."

"I should say it was," cut in Perry Larson, with emphasis. "An' strange ain't no name for it. One minute he'd be talking good common sense like anybody, and the next he'd be chatterin' of coats made o' ice, and birds and squirrels and babbling brooks. He sure is dippy! Listen. He actually don't seem to know the diff'rence between himself and his fiddle. We was tryin' to find out this mornin' what he could do, and what he wanted to do, when if he didn't up and say that his father told him it didn't make so much difference *what* he did so long as he kept hisself in tune and didn't strike false notes. Now, what do you think o' that?"

"Yes, I, know," said Higgins, nodding musingly. "There *was* something strange about them, and they weren't just ordinary tramps. Did I tell you? I overtook them last night away up on the Fairbanks road by the Taylor place, and I gave 'em a lift. I particularly noticed what a decent sort they were. They were clean and quiet-spoken, and their clothes were good, even if they were rough. Yet they didn't have any baggage but them fiddles."

"But what was that second letter you mentioned?" asked Simeon Holly.

Higgins smiled oddly, and reached into his pocket. "The letter? Oh, you're welcome to read the letter," he said, as he handed over a bit of folded paper.

Simeon took it gingerly and examined it.

It was a leaf torn apparently from a note book. It was folded three times and bore on the outside the superscription "To whom it may concern." The handwriting was peculiar, irregular, and not very legible. But as near as it could be deciphered, the note ran thus:

Now that the time has come when I must give David back to the world, I have set out for that purpose.

But I am ill—very ill, and should Death have swifter feet than I, I must leave my task for others to complete. Deal gently with him. He knows only that which is good and beautiful. He knows nothing of sin nor evil.

Then followed the signature—a thing of scrawls and flourishes that conveyed no sort of meaning to Simeon Holly's puzzled eyes.

"Well?" prompted Higgins expectantly.

Simeon Holly shook his head.

"I can make little of it. It certainly is a most remarkable note."

"Could you read the name?"

"No."

"Well, I couldn't either. Neither could half a dozen others that's seen it. But where's the boy? Maybe his note'll talk sense."

"I'll go find him," volunteered Larson. "He must be somewheres 'round."

But David was very evidently not "somewheres 'round." At least he was not in the barn, the shed, the kitchen bedroom, nor anywhere else that Larson looked; and the man was just coming back with a crestfallen, perplexed frown when Mrs. Holly hurried out on to the porch.

"Mr. Higgins," she cried, in obvious excitement, "your wife has just telephoned that her sister Mollie has just telephoned her that that little tramp boy with the violin is at her house."

"At Mollie's!" exclaimed Higgins. "Why, that's a mile or more from here."

"So that's where he is!" interposed Larson, hurrying forward. "Doggone the little rascal! He must 'a' slipped away while we was eatin' breakfast."

"Yes. But, Simeon—Mr. Higgins—we hadn't ought to let him go like that," appealed Mrs. Holly tremulously. "Your wife said Mollie said she found him crying at the crossroads, because he didn't know which way to take. He said he was going back home. He means to that wretched cabin on the mountain, you know;

and we can't let him do that alone—a child like that!"

"Where is he now?" demanded Higgins.

"In Mollie's kitchen eating bread and milk, but she said she had an awful time getting him to eat. And she wants to know what to do with him. That's why she telephoned your wife. She thought you ought to know he was there."

"Yes, of course. Well, tell her to tell him to come back."

"Mollie said she tried to have him come back, but that he said, no, thank you, he'd rather not. He was going home where his father could find him if he should ever want him. Mr. Higgins, we—we can't let him go off like that. Why, the child would die up there alone in those dreadful woods, even if he could get there in the first place—which I very much doubt."

"Yes, of course, of course," muttered Higgins, with a thoughtful frown. "There's his letter, too. Say!" he added, brightening. "What'll you bet that letter won't fetch him? He seems to think the world and all of his daddy. Here," he directed, turning to Mrs. Holly, "you tell my wife to tell—better yet, you telephone Mollie yourself, please, and tell her to tell the boy we've got a letter here for him from his father, and he can have it if he'll come back."

"I will, I will," called Mrs. Holly, over her shoulder, as she hurried into the house. In an unbelievably short time, she was back, her face beaming.

"He's started, so soon," she nodded. "He's crazy with joy, Mollie said. He even left part of his breakfast, he was in such a hurry. So I guess we'll see him all right."

"Oh, yes, we'll see him all right," echoed Simeon Holly grimly. "But that isn't telling what we'll do with him when we do see him."

"Oh, well, maybe this letter of his will help us out on that," suggested Higgins soothingly. "Anyhow, even if it doesn't, I'm not worrying any. I guess someone will want him—a good healthy boy like that."

"Did you find any money on the body?" asked Streeter.

"A little change—a few cents. Nothing to count. If the boy's letter doesn't tell us where any of their folks are, it'll be up to the town to bury him all right."

"He had a fiddle, didn't he? And the boy had one, too. Wouldn't they bring anything?" Streeter's round blue eyes gleamed shrewdly.

Higgins gave a slow shake of his head.

"Maybe—if there was a market for 'em. But who'd buy 'em? There ain't a soul in town plays but Jack Gurnsey, and he's got one. Besides, he's sick, and got all he can do to buy bread and butter for him and his sister without taking in more fiddles, I guess. HE wouldn't buy 'em."

"Hmm, maybe not, maybe not," grunted Streeter. "An', as you say, he's the only one that's got any use for them here; and like enough they ain't worth much, anyway. So I guess it is up to the town all right."

"Yes, but—if you'll take it from me," interrupted Larson, "you'll be wise if you keep still before the boy. It's no use asking him anything. We've proved that fast enough. And if he once turns 'round and begins to ask *you* questions, you're done for!"

"I guess you're right," nodded Higgins, with a quizzical smile. "And as long as questioning can't do any good, why, we'll just keep whist before the boy. Meanwhile, I wish the little rascal would hurry up and get here. I want to see the inside of that letter to him. I'm relying on that being some help to unsnarl this tangle of telling who they are."

"Well, he's started," reiterated Mrs. Holly, as she turned back toward the house, "so I guess he'll get here if you wait long enough."

"Oh, yes, he'll get here if we wait long enough," echoed Simeon Holly again, crustily.

The two men in the wagon settled themselves more comfortably in their seats, and Perry Larson, after a half-uneasy, half-apologetic glance at his employer, dropped himself onto the bottom step. Simeon Holly had already sat down stiffly in one of the porch chairs. Simeon Holly never "dropped himself" anywhere. Indeed, according to Perry Larson, if there were a hard way to do a thing, Simeon Holly found it—and did it. The fact that this morning he had allowed, and was still allowing, the sacred routine of the day's work to be thus interrupted, for nothing more important than the expected arrival of a strolling urchin, was something Larson would not have believed had he not seen it. Even now he was conscious, once or twice, of an involuntary desire to rub his eyes to make sure they were not deceiving him.

Impatient as the waiting men were for David's arrival, they were yet almost surprised at how soon he appeared running up the driveway.

"Oh, where is it, please?" he panted. "They said you had a letter for me from my daddy!"

"You're right, sonny, we have. And here it is," answered Higgins promptly, holding out the folded paper.

Plainly eager as he was, David did not open the note until he had first carefully set down the case holding his violin; then he devoured it with eager eyes.

As he read, the four men watched his face. They saw first the quick tears that had to be blinked away. Then they saw the radiant glow that grew and deepened until the whole boyish face was aflame with the splendor of it. They saw the shining wonder of his eyes, too, as he looked up from the letter.

"And Daddy wrote this to me from the far country?" he breathed.

Simeon Holly scowled. Larson choked over a stifled chuckle. William Streeter stared and shrugged his shoulders, but Higgins flushed a dull red.

"No, sonny," Higgins stammered. "We found it on the—er—I mean, it—er—your father left it in his pocket for you," finished the man, a little explosively.

A swift shadow crossed the boy's face. "Oh, I hoped I'd heard—" he began. Then suddenly he stopped, his face once more alight. "But it's 'most the same as if he wrote it from there, isn't it? He left it for me, and he told me what to do."

"What's that?" cried Higgins, instantly alert. "Did he tell you what to do? Then, let's have it, so we'll know. You will let us read it, won't you, boy?"

"Why, y—yes," stammered David, holding it out politely, but with evident reluctance.

"Thank you," said Higgins, as he reached for the note.

David's letter was very different from the other one. It was longer, but it did not help much, though it was easily read. In his letter, in spite of the wavering lines, each word was formed with a care that told of a father's thought for the young eyes that would read it. It was written on two of the notebook's leaves, and at the end came the single word "Daddy."

David, my boy [read Higgins aloud], in the far country I am waiting for you. Do not grieve, for that will grieve me. I shall not return, but some day you will come to me, your violin at your chin, and the bow drawn across the strings to greet me. See that it tells me of the beautiful world you have left—for it is a beautiful world, David; never forget that. And if sometime you are tempted to think it is not a beautiful world, just remember that you yourself can make it beautiful if you will.

You are among new faces, surrounded by things and people that are strange to you. Some of them you will not understand; some of them you may not like. But do not fear, David, and do not plead to go back to the hills. Remember this, my boy—in your violin lies all the things you long for. You have only to play and the broad skies of your mountain home will be over you, and the dear friends and comrades of your mountain forests will be about you.

Daddy

"That's worse than the other," groaned Higgins when he had finished the note. "There's actually nothing in it! Wouldn't you think—if a man wrote anything at such a time—that he'd 'a' wrote something that had some sense to it—something that one could get hold of, and find out who the boy is?"

There was no answering this. The assembled men could only grunt and nod in agreement, which, after all, was no real help.

CHAPTER 5

Discords

THE DEAD MAN FOUND IN FARMER HOLLY'S BARN CREATED a decided stir in the village of Hinsdale. The case was a peculiar one for many reasons. First, because of the boy—Hinsdale supposed it knew boys, but it felt inclined to change its mind after seeing this one. Second, because of the circumstances. The boy and his father had entered the town like tramps, yet Higgins, who talked freely of his having given the pair a "lift" on that very evening, did not hesitate to declare that he did not believe them to be ordinary tramps at all.

As there had been little found in the dead man's pockets, save the two notes, and as nobody could be found who wanted the violins, there seemed to be nothing to do but to turn the body over to the town for burial. Nothing was said of this to David. Indeed, as little as possible was said to David about anything after that morning when Higgins had given him his father's letter. At that time, the men had made one more effort to "get track of SOMETHING," as Higgins had despairingly put it. But the boy's answers to their questions were anything but satisfying, anything but helpful, and were often most disconcerting. The boy was, in fact, regarded by most of the men, after that morning, as being "a little off," and was hence let severely alone.

Who the man was the town authorities certainly did not know, neither could they apparently find out. His name, as written by himself, was unreadable. His notes told nothing; his son could tell little more—of consequence. A report, to be sure, did come from the village far up the mountain that such a man and boy had lived in a hut that was almost inaccessible, but even this did not help solve the mystery.

David was left at the Holly farmhouse, though Simeon Holly mentally declared that he should lose no time in looking about for someone to take the boy away.

On that first day, Higgins, picking up the reins preparatory to driving from the yard, had said, with a nod of his head toward David, "Well, how about it, Holly? Shall we leave him here until we find somebody that wants him?"

"Why, y—yes, I suppose so," hesitated Simeon Holly, with an uncordial accent.

But his wife, hovering in the background, hastened forward at once. "Oh, yes; yes, indeed," she urged. "I'm sure he—he won't be a mite of trouble, Simeon."

"Perhaps not," conceded Simeon Holly darkly. "Neither, it is safe to say, will he be anything else—worth anything."

"That's it exactly," spoke up Streeter, from his seat in the wagon. "If I thought he'd be worth his salt, now, I'd take him myself; but— well, look at him this minute," he finished, with a disdainful shrug.

David, on the lowest step, was very evidently not hearing a word of what was being said. With his sensitive face illumined, he was again poring over his father's letter.

Something in the sudden quiet cut through his absorption as the noisy hum of voices had not been able to do, and he raised his head. His eyes were star like.

"I'm so glad Father told me what to do," he breathed. "It'll be easier now."

Receiving no answer from the somewhat awkwardly silent men, he went on, as if in explanation, "You know he's waiting for me—in the far country, I mean. He said he was. And when you've got somebody waiting, you don't mind staying behind yourself for a little while. Besides, I've *got* to stay to find out about the beautiful world, you know, so I can tell him, when I go. That's the way I used to do back home on the mountain, you see—tell him about things. Lots of days we'd go to walk; then, when we got home, he'd have me tell him, with my violin, what I'd seen. And now he says I'm to stay here."

"Here!" It was the quick, stern voice of Simeon Holly.

"Yes," nodded David earnestly; "to learn about the beautiful world. Don't you remember? And he said I was not to want to go back to my mountains; that I would not need to, anyway, because the mountains, and the sky, and the birds and squirrels and brooks are really in my violin, you know. And—" But with an angry frown, Simeon Holly stalked away, motioning Larson to follow him. And with a merry glance and a low chuckle, Higgins turned his horse about and drove from the yard. A moment later, David found himself alone with Mrs. Holly, who was looking at him with wistful, though slightly fearful eyes.

"Did you have all the breakfast you wanted?" she asked timidly, resorting, as she had resorted the night before, to the everyday things of her world in the hope that they might make this strange little boy seem less wild, and more nearly human.

"Oh, yes, thank you." David's eyes had strayed back to the note in his hand. Suddenly, he looked up, a new something in his eyes. "What is it to be a—a tramp?" he asked. "Those men said Daddy and I were tramps."

"A tramp? Oh—er—why, just a—a tramp," stammered Mrs. Holly. "But never mind that, David. I—I wouldn't think any more about it."

"But what *is* a tramp?" persisted David, a smoldering fire beginning to show in his eyes. "Because if they meant *thieves*—"

"No, no, David," interrupted Mrs. Holly soothingly. "They never meant thieves at all."

"Then, what is it to be a tramp?"

"Why, it's just to—to tramp," explained Mrs. Holly desperately, "to walk along the road from one town to another, and—and not live in a house at all."

"Oh!" David's face cleared. "That's all right, then. I'd love to be a tramp, and so would Father. And we were tramps, sometimes, too, 'cause lots of times, in the summer, we didn't stay in the cabin hardly any—just lived out of doors all day and all night. Why, I never knew really what the pine trees were saying till I heard them at night, lying under them. You know what I mean. You've heard them, haven't you?"

"At night? Pine trees?" stammered Mrs. Holly helplessly.

"Yes. Oh, haven't you ever heard them at night?" cried the boy, in his voice a very genuine sympathy as for a grievous loss. "Why, then, if you've only heard them daytimes, you don't know a bit what pine trees really are. But I can tell you. Listen! This is what they say," finished the boy, whipping his violin from its case, and, after a swift testing of the strings, plunging into a weird, haunting little melody.

In the doorway, Mrs. Holly, bewildered yet bewitched, stood motionless, her eyes half-fearfully, half-longingly fixed on David's glorified face. She was still in the same position when Simeon Holly came around the corner of the house.

"Well, Ellen," he began, with quiet scorn, after a moment's stern watching of the scene before him, "have you nothing better to do this morning than to listen to this minstrel fellow?"

"Oh, Simeon! Why, yes, of course. I—I forgot—what I was doing," faltered Mrs. Holly, flushing guiltily from neck to brow as she turned and hurried into the house.

David, on the porch steps, seemed to have heard nothing. He

was still playing, his rapt gaze on the distant skyline, when Simeon Holly turned upon him with disapproving eyes.

"See here, boy, can't you do anything but fiddle?" he demanded. Then, as David still continued to play, he added sharply: "Didn't you hear me, boy?"

The music stopped abruptly. David looked up with the slightly dazed air of one who has been summoned as from another world. "Did you speak to me, sir?" he asked.

"I did—twice. I asked if you never did anything but play that fiddle."

"You mean at home?" David's face expressed mild wonder without a trace of anger or resentment. "Why, yes, of course. I couldn't play ALL the time, you know. I had to eat and sleep and study my books; and every day we went to walk—like tramps, as you call them," he elucidated, his face brightening with obvious delight at being able, for once, to explain matters in terms that he felt sure would be understood.

"Tramps, indeed!" muttered Simeon Holly, under his breath. Then, sharply: "Did you never perform any useful labor, boy? Were your days always spent in this ungodly idleness?"

Again David frowned in mild wonder. "Oh, I wasn't idle, sir. Father said I must never be that. He said every instrument was needed in the great Orchestra of Life, and that I was one, you know, even if I was only a little boy. And he said if I kept still and didn't do my part, the harmony wouldn't be complete, and—"

"Yes, yes, but never mind that now, boy," interrupted Simeon Holly, with harsh impatience. "I mean, did he never set you to work—real work?"

"Work?" David meditated again. Then suddenly his face cleared. "Oh, yes, sir. He said I had a beautiful work to do, and that it was waiting for me out in the world. That's why we came down from the mountain, you know, to find it. Is that what you mean?"

"Well, no," retorted the man, "I can't say that it was. I was referring to work—real work about the house. Did you never do any of that?"

David gave a relieved laugh. "Oh, you mean getting the meals and tidying up the house," he replied. "Oh, yes, I did that with Father, only—" His face grew wistful. "I'm afraid I didn't do it very well. My bacon was never as nice and crisp as Father's, and the fire was always spoiling my potatoes."

"Humph! Bacon and potatoes, indeed!" scorned Simeon Holly. "Well, boy, we call that women's work down here. We set men to something else. Do you see that woodpile by the shed door?"

"Yes, sir."

"Very good. In the kitchen you'll find an empty wood box. Do you think you could fill it with wood from that woodpile? You'll find plenty of short, small sticks already chopped."

"Oh, yes, sir, I'd like to," said David, hastily but carefully tucking his violin into its case. A minute later, he had attacked the woodpile with a will; and Simeon Holly, after a sharply watchful glance, had turned away.

But the wood box, after all, was not filled. At least, it was not filled immediately, for at the very beginning of gathering the second armful of wood, David picked up a stick that had long lain in one position on the ground, thereby disclosing sundry and diverse crawling things of many legs, which filled David's soul with delight and drove away every thought of the empty wood box.

It was only a matter of some strength and more patience, and still more time, to overturn other and bigger sticks, to find other and bigger of the many-legged, many-jointed creatures. One, indeed, was so very wonderful that David, with a whoop of glee, summoned Mrs. Holly from the shed doorway to come and see.

So urgent was his plea that Mrs. Holly came with hurried steps—but she went away with steps even more hurried; and

David, sitting back on his woodpile seat, was left to wonder why she should scream and shudder and say "Ugh!" at such a beautiful, interesting thing as was this little creature who lived in her woodpile.

Even then David did not think of that empty wood box waiting behind the kitchen stove. This time it was a butterfly, a big black butterfly banded with gold; and it danced and fluttered all through the backyard and out into the garden, David delightedly following with soft-treading steps and movements that would not startle. From the garden to the orchard, and from the orchard back to the garden, danced the butterfly—and David! And in the garden, near the house, David came upon Mrs. Holly's pansy bed. Even the butterfly was forgotten then, for down in the path by the pansy bed, David dropped to his knees in veritable worship.

"Why, you're just like little people," he cried softly. "You've got faces; and some of you are happy, and some of you are sad. And you—you big spotted yellow one—you're laughing at me. Oh, I'm going to play you—all of you. You'll make such a pretty song, you're so different from each other!" And David leaped lightly to his feet and ran around to the side porch for his violin.

Five minutes later, Simeon Holly, coming into the kitchen, heard the sound of a violin through the open window. At the same moment his eyes fell on the wood box, empty save for a few small sticks at the bottom. With an angry frown, he strode through the outer door and around the corner of the house to the garden. At once, then, he came upon David, sitting Turk-fashion in the middle of the path before the pansy bed, his violin at his chin and his whole face aglow.

"Well, boy, is this the way you fill the wood box?" demanded the man crisply.

David shook his head. "Oh, no, sir, this isn't filling the wood box," he laughed, softening his music but not stopping it. "Did

you think that was what I was playing? It's the flowers here that
I'm playing—the little faces, like people, you know. See, this is that
big yellow one over there that's laughing," he finished, letting the
music under his fingers burst into a gay little melody.

Simeon Holly raised an imperious hand; and at the gesture,
David stopped his melody in the middle of a run, his eyes flying
wide open in plain wonderment.

"You mean—I'm not playing—right?" he asked.

"I'm not talking of your playing," retorted Simeon Holly
severely. "I'm talking of that wood box I asked you to fill."

David's face cleared. "Oh, yes, sir. I'll go and do it," he nodded,
getting cheerfully to his feet.

"But I told you to do it before."

David's eyes grew puzzled again. "I know, sir, and I started to,"
he answered, with the obvious patience of one who finds himself
obliged to explain what should be a self-evident fact, "but I saw so
many beautiful things, one after another, and when I found these
funny little flower-people I just had to play them. Don't you see?"

"No, I can't say that I do, when I'd already told you to fill the
wood box," rejoined the man, with uncompromising coldness.

"You mean, even then, that I ought to have filled the wood box
first?"

"I certainly do."

David's eyes flew wide open again. "But my song—I'd have
lost it!" he exclaimed. "And Father said always when a song came
to me to play it at once. Songs are like the mists of the morning
and the rainbows, you know, and they don't stay with you long.
You just have to catch them quick, before they go. Now, don't you
see?"

But Simeon Holly, with a despairingly scornful gesture, had
turned away; and David, after a moment's following him with
wistful eyes, soberly walked toward the kitchen door. Two minutes

later, he was industriously working at his task of filling the wood box.

That for David the affair was not satisfactorily settled was evidenced by his thoughtful countenance and preoccupied air, however. Nor were matters helped any by the question David put to Mr. Holly just before dinner.

"Do you mean," he asked, "that because I didn't fill the wood box right away, I was being a discord?"

"You were what?" demanded the amazed Simeon Holly.

"Being a discord—playing out of tune, you know," explained David, with patient earnestness. "Father said—" But again Simeon Holly had turned irritably away, and David was left with his perplexed questions still unanswered.

CHAPTER 6

Nuisances, Necessary and Otherwise

FOR SOME TIME AFTER DINNER THAT FIRST DAY, DAVID watched Mrs. Holly in silence while she cleared the table and began to wash the dishes.

"Do you want me to—help?" he asked at last, a little wistfully.

Mrs. Holly, with a dubious glance at the boy's brown little hands, shook her head. "No, I don't. No, thank you," she amended her answer.

For another sixty seconds David was silent. Then, still more wistfully, he asked, "Are all these things you've been doing all day 'useful labor'?"

Mrs. Holly lifted dripping hands from the dishpan and held them suspended for an amazed instant. "Are they— Why, of course they are! What a silly question! What put that idea into your head, child?"

"Mr. Holly; and you see it's so different from what Father used to call them."

"Different?"

"Yes. He said they were a necessary nuisance—dishes, and getting meals, and clearing up—and he didn't do half as many of them as you do, either."

"Nuisance, indeed!" Mrs. Holly resumed her dish washing with some asperity. "Well, I should think that might have been just about like him."

"Yes, it was. He was always that way," nodded David pleasantly. Then after a moment, he queried: "But aren't you going to walk at all today?"

"To walk? Where?"

"Why, through the woods and fields—anywhere."

"Walking in the woods, now—*just walking*? Land's sake, boy, I've got something else to do!"

"Oh, that's too bad, isn't it?" David's face expressed sympathetic regret. "And it's such a nice day! Maybe it'll rain by tomorrow."

"Maybe it will," retorted Mrs. Holly, with slightly uplifted eyebrows and an expressive glance. "But whether it does or doesn't won't make any difference in my going to walk, I guess."

"Oh, won't it?" beamed David, his face changing. "I'm so glad! I don't mind the rain, either. Father and I used to go in the rain lots of times, only, of course, we couldn't take our violins then, so we used to like the pleasant days better. But there are some things you find on rainy days that you can't find any other time, aren't there? The dance of the drops on the leaves, and the rush of the rain when the wind gets behind it. Don't you love to feel it, out in the open spaces, where the wind just gets a good chance to push?"

Mrs. Holly stared. Then she shivered and threw up her hands with a gesture of hopeless abandonment. "Land's sake, boy!" she said feebly, as she turned back to her work.

Mrs. Holly hurried from dishes to sweeping, and from sweeping to dusting, going at last into the somber parlor, always carefully guarded from sun and air. Watching her mutely, David trailed behind, his eyes staring a little as they fell upon the multitude of objects that the parlor contained: the haircloth chairs; the long sofa; the marble-topped table; the curtains, cushions, spreads, and "throws"; the innumerable mats and tidies; the hair-wreath; the wax flowers under their glass dome; the dried grasses; the marvelous bouquets of scarlet, green, and purple everlastings; the stones and shells and many-sized, many-shaped vases arranged as if in line of battle along the corner shelves.

"Y—yes, you may come in," called Mrs. Holly, glancing back at the hesitating boy in the doorway. "But you mustn't touch anything. I'm going to dust."

"But I haven't seen this room before," ruminated David.

"Well, no," deigned Mrs. Holly, with just a touch of superiority. "We don't use this room common, little boy, nor the bedroom there, either. This is the company room, for ministers and funerals, and—" She stopped hastily, with a quick look at David, but the boy did not seem to have heard.

"And doesn't anybody live here in this house but just you and Mr. Holly and Mr. Perry Larson?" he asked, still looking wonderingly about him.

"No, not—now." Mrs. Holly drew in her breath with a little catch, and glanced at the framed portrait of a little boy on the wall.

"But you've got such a lot of rooms and—and things," remarked David. "Why, Daddy and I only had two rooms, and not hardly any *things*. It was so—different, you know, in my home."

"I should say it might have been!" Mrs. Holly began to dust hurriedly, but carefully. Her voice still carried its hint of superiority.

"Oh, yes," smiled David. "But you say you don't use this room much, so that helps."

"Helps!" In her stupefaction Mrs. Holly stopped her work and stared.

"Why, yes. I mean, you've got so many other rooms, you can live in those. You don't *have* to live in here."

"'Have to live in here'!" ejaculated the woman, still too uncomprehending to be anything but amazed.

"Yes. But do you have to *keep* all these things, and clean them and clean them, like this, every day? Couldn't you give them to somebody, or throw them away?"

"Throw—these—things—away!" With a wild sweep of her arms, the horrified woman seemed to be trying to encompass in a protective embrace each last endangered treasure of mat and tidy. "Boy, are you crazy? These things are—are valuable. They cost money, and time, and—and labor. Don't you know beautiful things when you see them?"

"Oh, yes, I love *beautiful* things," smiled David, with unconsciously rude emphasis. "And up on the mountain, I had them always. There was the sunrise and the sunset, and the moon and the stars, and my Silver Lake, and the cloud-boats that sailed—"

But Mrs. Holly, with a vexed gesture, stopped him.

"Never mind, little boy. I might have known—brought up as you have been. Of course, you could not appreciate such things as these. Throw them away, indeed!" And she fell to work again, but this time her fingers carried a something in their touch that was almost like the caress a mother might bestow upon an aggrieved child.

David, vaguely disturbed and uncomfortable, watched her with troubled eyes; then, apologetically, he explained, "It was only that I thought if you didn't have to clean so many of these things, you could maybe go to walk more—today, and other days, you know. You said you didn't have time," he reminded her.

But Mrs. Holly only shook her head and sighed, "Well, well, never mind, little boy. I dare say you meant all right. You couldn't understand, of course."

And David, after another moment's wistful eying of the caressing fingers, turned about and wandered out onto the side porch. A minute later, having seated himself on the porch steps, he had taken from his pocket two small pieces of folded paper. And then, through tear-dimmed eyes, he read once more his father's letter.

"He said I mustn't grieve, for that would grieve him," murmured the boy after a time, his eyes on the far-away hills. "And he said if I'd play, my mountains would come to me here, and I'd really be at home up there. He said in my violin were all those things I'm wanting—so bad!"

With a little choking breath, David tucked the note back into his pocket and reached for his violin.

Some time later, Mrs. Holly, dusting the chairs in the parlor, stopped her work, tiptoed to the door, and listened breathlessly. When she turned back, still later, to her work, her eyes were wet.

"I wonder why, when he plays, I always get to thinking of John," she sighed to herself, as she picked up her dusting-cloth.

After supper that night, Simeon Holly and his wife again sat on the kitchen porch, resting from the labor of the day. Simeon's eyes were closed. His wife's were on the dim outlines of the shed, the barn, the road, or a passing horse and wagon. David, sitting on the steps, was watching the moon climb higher and higher above the treetops. After a while, he slipped into the house and came out with his violin.

At the first long-drawn note of sweetness, Simeon Holly opened his eyes and sat up, stern-lipped. But his wife laid a timid hand on his arm.

"Don't say anything, please," she entreated softly. "Let him play, just for tonight. He's lonesome—poor little fellow." And Simeon Holly, with a frowning shrug of his shoulders, sat back in his chair.

Later, it was Mrs. Holly herself who stopped the music by saying: "Come, David, it's bedtime for little boys. I'll go upstairs with you." And she led the way into the house and lighted the candle for him.

Upstairs, in the little room over the kitchen, David found himself once more alone. As before, the little yellow-white nightshirt lay over the chair-back; and as before, Mrs. Holly had brushed away a tear as she had placed it there. As before, too, the big four-posted bed loomed tall and formidable in the corner. But this time the coverlet and sheet were turned back invitingly—Mrs. Holly had been much disturbed to find that David had slept on the floor the night before.

Once more, with his back carefully turned toward the impaled bugs and moths on the wall, David undressed himself. Then, before blowing out the candle, he went to the window, knelt down, and looked up at the moon through the trees.

David was sorely puzzled. He was beginning to wonder just what was to become of himself.

His father had said that out in the world there was a beautiful work for him to do; but what was it? How was he to find it? Or how was he to do it if he did find it? And another thing; where was he to live? Could he stay where he was? It was not home, to be sure; but there was the little room over the kitchen where he might sleep, and there was the kind woman who smiled at him sometimes with the sad, far-away look in her eyes that somehow hurt. He would not like, now, to leave her—with Daddy gone.

There were the gold pieces, too; and concerning these David was equally puzzled. What should he do with them? He did not need them. The kind woman was giving him plenty of food so that he did not have to go to the store and buy; and there was nothing else, apparently, that he could use them for. They were heavy and disagreeable to carry; yet he did not like to throw them away, nor to let anybody know that he had them. He had been called a thief just for one little piece, and what would they say if they knew he had all those others?

David remembered now, suddenly, that his father had said to hide them—to hide them until he needed them. David was relieved at once. Why had he not thought of it before? He knew just the place, too—the little cupboard behind the chimney there in this very room! And with a satisfied sigh, David got to his feet, gathered all the little yellow disks from his pockets, and tucked them well out of sight behind the piles of books on the cupboard shelves. There, too, he hid the watch; but he slipped the little miniature of the angel-mother back into one of his pockets.

David's second morning at the farmhouse was not unlike the first, except that this time, when Simeon Holly asked him to fill the wood box, David resolutely ignored every enticing bug and butterfly and kept rigorously to the task before him until it was done.

He was in the kitchen when, just before dinner, Perry Larson came into the room with a worried frown on his face. "Mis' Holly, would ye mind just stepping to the side door? There's a woman and a little boy there, and something ails 'em. She can't talk English, and I'm blest if I can make head nor tail out of the lingo she *does* talk. But maybe you can."

"Why, Perry, I don't know—" began Mrs. Holly. But she turned at once toward the door.

On the porch steps stood a very pretty but frightened-looking young woman with a boy perhaps ten years old at her side. Upon catching sight of Mrs. Holly, she burst into a torrent of unintelligible words, supplemented by numerous and vehement gestures.

Mrs. Holly shrank back and cast appealing eyes toward her husband, who at that moment had come across the yard from the barn. "Simeon, can you tell what she wants?"

At sight of the newcomer on the scene, the strange woman began again, with even more volubility.

"No," said Simeon Holly, after a moment's scowling scrutiny of the gesticulating woman. "She's talking French, I think. And she wants—something."

"I should say she did," muttered Perry Larson. "An' whatever it is, she wants it powerful bad."

"Are you hungry?" questioned Mrs. Holly timidly.

"Can't you speak English at all?" demanded Simeon Holly.

The woman looked from one to the other with the piteous, pleading eyes of the stranger in the strange land who cannot understand or make others understand. She had turned away with a despairing shake of her head, when suddenly she gave a wild cry of joy and wheeled about, her whole face alight.

The Hollys and Perry Larson saw then that David had come out onto the porch and was speaking to the woman—and his words were just as unintelligible as the woman's had been.

Mrs. Holly and Perry Larson stared. Simeon Holly interrupted David with a sharp "Do you understand this woman, boy?"

"Why, yes! Didn't you? She's lost her way, and—" But the woman had hurried forward and was pouring her story into David's ears. At its conclusion, David turned to find the look of stupefaction still on the others' faces.

"Well, what does she want?" asked Simeon Holly crisply.

"She wants to find the way to Francois Lavelle's house. He's her husband's brother. She came in on the train this morning. Her husband stopped off a minute somewhere, she says, and got left behind. He could talk English, but she can't. She's only been in this country a week. She came from France."

"Won't ye listen to that, now?" cried Perry Larson admiringly. "Reads her just like a book, don't he? There's a French family over in West Hinsdale—two of 'em, I think. What'll ye bet 't ain't one o' them?"

"Very likely," acceded Simeon Holly, his eyes bent disapprovingly on David's face. It was plain to be seen that Simeon Holly's attention was occupied by David, not the woman.

"An', say, Mr. Holly," resumed Perry Larson, a little excitedly, "you know I was going' over to West Hinsdale in a day or two to see Harlow about them steers. Why can't I go this afternoon and tote her and the kid along?"

"Very well," nodded Simeon Holly curtly, his eyes still on David's face.

Perry Larson turned to the woman, and by a flourish of his arms and a jumble of broken English attempted to make her understand that he was to take her where she undoubtedly wished to go. The woman still looked uncomprehending, however, and David promptly came to the rescue, saying a few rapid words that quickly brought a flood of delighted understanding to the woman's face.

"Can't you ask her if she's hungry?" ventured Mrs. Holly.

"She says no, thank you," translated David, with a smile, when he had received his answer. "But the boy says he is, if you please."

"Then, tell them to come into the kitchen," directed Mrs. Holly, hurrying into the house.

"So you're French, are you?" said Simeon Holly to David.

"French? Oh, no, sir," smiled David, proudly. "I'm an American. Father said I was. He said I was born in this country."

"But how comes it you can speak French like that?"

"Why, I learned it." Then, divining that his words were still unconvincing, he added, "Same as I learned German and other things with Father, out of books, you know. Didn't you learn French when you were a little boy?"

"Humph!" vouchsafed Simeon Holly, stalking away without answering the question.

Immediately after dinner, Perry Larson drove away with the woman and the little boy. The woman's face was wreathed with smiles, and her last adoring glance was for David, who was waving his hand to her from the porch steps.

In the afternoon David took his violin and went off toward the hill behind the house for a walk. He had asked Mrs. Holly to accompany him, but she had refused, though she was not sweeping or dusting at the time. She was doing nothing more important, apparently, than making holes in a piece of white cloth, and sewing them up again with a needle and thread.

David had then asked Mr. Holly to go; but his refusal was even more strangely impatient than his wife's had been. "And why, pray, should I go for a useless walk now—or any time, for that matter?" he demanded sharply.

David had shrunk back unconsciously, though he had still smiled. "Oh, but it wouldn't be a useless walk, sir. Father said nothing was useless that helped to keep us in tune, you know."

"In tune!"

"I mean, you looked as Father used to look sometimes, when he felt out of tune. And he always said there was nothing like a walk to put him back again. I—I was feeling a little out of tune myself today, and I thought, by the way you looked, that you were, too. So I asked you to go to walk."

"Humph! Well, I— That will do, boy. No impertinence, you understand!" And he had turned away in very obvious anger.

David, with a puzzled sorrow in his heart, had started alone then, on his walk.

Chapter 7

"You're Wanted! — You're Wanted!"

IT WAS SATURDAY NIGHT AND THE END OF DAVID'S THIRD DAY at the farmhouse. Upstairs, in the hot little room over the kitchen, the boy knelt at the window and tried to find a breath of cool air from the hills. Downstairs on the porch, Simeon Holly and his wife discussed the events of the past few days and talked of what should be done with David.

"But what shall we do with him?" moaned Mrs. Holly, at last breaking a long silence that had fallen between them. "What can we do with him? Doesn't anybody want him?"

"No, of course, nobody wants him," retorted her husband relentlessly.

And at the words, a small figure in a yellow-white nightshirt stopped short. David, violin in hand, had fled from the little hot room and stood now just inside the kitchen door.

"Who can want a child that has been brought up in that heathenish fashion?" continued Simeon Holly. "According to his own story, even his father did nothing but play the fiddle and tramp through the woods day in and day out, with an occasional trip to the mountain village to get food and clothing when they had absolutely nothing to eat and wear. Of course nobody wants him!"

David, at the kitchen door, caught his breath chokingly. Then he sped across the floor to the back hall, and then on through the long sheds to the hayloft in the barn—the place where his father always seemed nearest.

David was frightened and heartsick. Nobody wanted him. He had heard it with his own ears, so there was no mistake. Now what about all those long days and nights ahead before he might go, violin in hand, to meet his father in that far-away country? How was he to live those days and nights if nobody wanted him? How was his violin to speak in a voice that was true and pure and full, and tell of the beautiful world as his father had said that it must do? David quite cried aloud at the thought. Then he thought of something else that his father had said: "Remember this, my boy— in your violin lie all the things you long for. You have only to play, and the broad skies of your mountain home will be over you, and the dear friends and comrades of your mountain forests will be all about you." With a quick cry, David raised his violin and drew the bow across the strings.

Back on the porch at that moment Mrs. Holly was saying, "Of course there's the orphan asylum, or maybe the poorhouse, if they'd take him, but—" She broke off sharply. "Simeon, where's that child playing now?"

Simeon listened with intent ears. "In the barn, I should say."

"But he'd gone to bed!"

"And he'll go to bed again," asserted Simeon Holly grimly, as he rose to his feet and stalked across the moonlit yard to the barn.

As before, Mrs. Holly followed him, and as before, both involuntarily paused just inside the barn door to listen. No runs and trills and rollicking bits of melody floated down the stairway tonight. The notes were long-drawn and plaintively sweet, and they rose and swelled and died almost into silence while the man and the woman by the door stood listening.

They were back in the long ago—Simeon Holly and his wife— back with a boy of their own who had made those same rafters

ring with shouts of laughter, and who also had played the violin—
though not like this; and the same thought had come to each:
"What if, after all, it were John playing all alone in the moonlight!"

It had not been the violin, in the end, that had driven John
Holly from home. It had been the possibilities in a piece of crayon.
All through childhood the boy had drawn his beloved "pictures"
on every inviting space that offered—whether it was the "best-
room" wallpaper or the flyleaf of the big plush album—and at
eighteen, he had announced his determination to be an artist. For
a year after that Simeon Holly fought with all the strength of a
stubborn will, banished chalk and crayon from the house, and set
the boy to homely tasks that left no time for anything but food and
sleep. Then John ran away.

That was fifteen years ago, and they had not seen him since;
though two unanswered letters in Simeon Holly's desk testified
that perhaps this, at least, was not the boy's fault.

It was not of the grown-up John, the willful boy and runaway
son, however, that Simeon Holly and his wife were thinking of as
they stood just inside the barn door; it was of baby John, the little
curly-headed fellow that had played at their knees, frolicked in this
very barn, and nestled in their arms when the day was done.

Mrs. Holly spoke first, and it was not as she had spoken on the
porch.

"Simeon," she began tremulously, "that dear child must go to
bed!" And she hurried across the floor and up the stairs, followed
by her husband. "Come, David," she said, as she reached the top.
"It's time little boys were asleep! Come!"

Her voice was low, and not quite steady. To David, her voice
sounded as her eyes looked when there was in them the far-away
something that hurt. Very slowly he came forward into the
moonlight, his gaze searching the woman's face long and earnestly.

"And do you—want me?" he faltered.

The woman drew in her breath with a little sob. Before her stood the slender figure in the yellow-white gown—John's gown. Into her eyes looked those other eyes, dark and wistful—like John's eyes. And her arms ached with emptiness.

"Yes, yes, for my very own—and for always!" she cried with sudden passion, clasping the little form close. "For always!"

And David sighed his content.

Simeon Holly's lips parted, but they closed again with no words said. The man turned then, with a curiously baffled look, and stalked down the stairs.

On the porch long minutes later, when once more David had gone to bed, Simeon Holly said coldly to his wife, "I suppose you realize, Ellen, just what you've pledged yourself to, by that absurd outburst of yours in the barn tonight—and all because that ungodly music and the moonshine had gone to your head!"

"But I want the boy, Simeon. He, he makes me think of—John."

Harsh lines came to the man's mouth, but there was a perceptible shake in his voice as he answered, "We're not talking about John, Ellen. We're talking about this irresponsible, hardly sane boy upstairs. He can work, I suppose, if he's taught; and in that way, he won't perhaps be a dead loss. Still, he's another mouth to feed, and that counts now. There's the note, you know. It's due in August."

"But you say there's money—almost enough for it—in the bank." Mrs. Holly's voice was anxiously apologetic.

"Yes, I know," vouchsafed the man. "But almost enough is not quite enough."

"But there's time, more than two months. It isn't due till the last of August, Simeon."

"I know, I know. Meanwhile, there's the boy. What are you going to do with him?"

"Why, can't you use him on the farm a little?"

"Perhaps. I doubt it, though," said the man gloomily. "One can't hoe corn nor pull weeds with a fiddle-bow, and that's all he seems to know how to handle."

"But he can learn, and he does play beautifully."

There was no reply except a muttered "Humph!" under the breath. Then Simeon Holly rose and stalked into the house.

The next day was Sunday, and Sunday at the farmhouse was a thing of stern repression and solemn silence. In Simeon Holly's veins ran the blood of the Puritans, and he was more than strict as to what he considered right and wrong. When half-trained for the ministry, ill-health had forced him to resort to a less confining life, though it had never taken from him the uncompromising rigor of his views. It was a distinct shock to him, therefore, on this Sunday morning to be awakened by a peal of music such as the little house had never known before. All the while that he was thrusting his indignant self into his clothing, the runs and turns and crashing chords whirled about him until it seemed that a whole orchestra must be imprisoned in the little room over the kitchen, so skillful was the boy's double stopping. Simeon Holly was white with anger when he finally hurried down the hall and threw open David's bedroom door.

"Boy, what do you mean by this?" he demanded.

David laughed gleefully. "Didn't you know?" he asked. "Why, I thought my music would tell you. I was so happy, so glad! The birds in the trees woke me up singing, 'You're wanted—you're wanted!' And the sun came over the hill there and said, 'You're wanted—you're wanted!' And the little tree branch tapped on my window pane and said, 'You're wanted—you're wanted!' And I just had to take up my violin and tell you about it!"

"But it's Sunday—the Lord's Day," remonstrated the man sternly.

David stood motionless, his eyes questioning.

"Are you quite a heathen, then?" asked the man sharply. "Have they never told you anything about God, boy?"

"Oh, 'God'?—of course," smiled David, in open relief. "God wraps up the buds in their little brown blankets, and covers the roots with—"

"I am not talking about brown blankets nor roots," interrupted the man severely. "This is God's day, and as such should be kept holy."

"'Holy'?"

"Yes. You should not fiddle nor laugh nor sing."

"But those are good things, and beautiful things," defended David, his eyes wide and puzzled.

"In their place, perhaps," conceded the man, stiffly, "but not on God's day."

"You mean—He wouldn't like them?"

"Yes."

"Oh!" And David's face cleared. "That's all right, then. Your God isn't the same one, sir, for mine loves all beautiful things every day in the year."

There was a moment's silence. For the first time in his life, Simeon Holly found himself without words.

"We won't talk of this anymore, David," he said at last, "but we'll put it another way: I don't wish you to play your fiddle on Sunday. Now, put it up till tomorrow." And he turned and went down the hall.

Breakfast was a very quiet meal that morning. Meals were never things of hilarious joy at the Holly farmhouse, as David had already found out, but he had not seen one before quite so somber as this. It was followed immediately by a half-hour of scripture reading and prayer, with Mrs. Holly and Perry Larson sitting very stiff and solemn in their chairs, while Mr. Holly read. David tried to sit very stiff and solemn in his chair, also; but the roses at the window were nodding their heads and beckoning; and the birds in the bushes beyond were sending to him coaxing little chirps of "Come out, come out!" And how could one expect to sit stiff and solemn in the face of all that, particularly when one's fingers were tingling to take up the interrupted song of the morning and tell the whole world how beautiful it was to be wanted!

Yet David sat very still—or as still as he could sit—and only the tapping of his foot and the roving of his wistful eyes told that his mind was not with Farmer Holly.

After the devotions came an hour of subdued haste and confusion while the family prepared for church. David had never been to church. He asked Perry Larson what it was like, but Perry only shrugged his shoulders and said, to nobody, apparently, "Sugar! Won't ye hear that, now?"—which to David was certainly no answer at all.

David soon found out that one must be spick and span to go to church. Never before had he been so scrubbed and brushed and combed. There was, too, a little clean white blouse and a red tie brought out for him to wear, over which Mrs. Holly cried a little as she had over the nightshirt that first evening.

The church was in the village only a quarter of a mile away; and in due time David, open-eyed and interested, was following Mr. and Mrs. Holly down its long center aisle. The Hollys were early as usual, and service had not begun. Even the organist had not taken his seat beneath the great pipes of blue and gold that towered to the ceiling.

It was the pride of the town—that organ. It had been given by a great man (out in the world) whose birthplace the town was. More than that, a yearly donation from this same great man paid for the skilled organist who came every Sunday from the city to play it. Today, as the organist took his seat, he noticed a new face in the Holly pew, and he almost gave a friendly smile as he met the wondering gaze of the small boy there; then he lost himself, as usual, in the music before him.

Down in the Holly pew, the small boy held his breath. A score of violins was singing in his ears, and a score of other instruments that he could not name crashed over his head and brought him to his feet in ecstasy. Before a detaining hand could stop him, he was out in the aisle, his eyes on the blue and gold pipes from which seemed to come those wondrous sounds. Then his gaze fell on the man and on the banks of keys, and with soft steps, he crept along the aisle and up the stairs to the organ loft.

For long minutes he stood motionless, listening; then the music died into silence and the minister rose for the invocation. It was a boy's voice and not a man's, however, that broke the pause.

"Oh, sir, please," it said, "would you—could you teach *me* to do that?"

The organist choked over a cough, and the soprano reached out and drew David to her side, whispering something in his ear. The minister, after a dazed silence, bowed his head; while down in the Holly pew an angry man and a sorely mortified woman vowed that, before David came to church again, he should have learned some things.

CHAPTER 8

The Puzzling "Do's" and "Don'ts"

WITH THE COMING OF MONDAY ARRIVED A NEW LIFE for David—a curious life full of "don'ts" and "do's." David wondered sometimes why all the pleasant things were "don'ts" and all the unpleasant ones "do's." Corn to be hoed, weeds to be pulled, wood boxes to be filled; with all these it was "do this, do this, do this." But when it came to lying under the apple trees, exploring the brook that ran by the field, or even watching the bugs and worms that one found in the earth—all these were "don'ts."

As to Farmer Holly—Farmer Holly himself awoke to some new experiences that Monday morning. One of them was the difficulty in successfully combating the cheerfully expressed opinion that weeds were so pretty growing that it was a pity to pull them up and let them all wither and die. Another was the equally great difficulty of keeping a small boy at useful labor of any sort in the face of the attractions displayed by a passing cloud, a blossoming shrub, or a bird singing on a tree branch.

In spite of all this, however, David so evidently did his best to carry out the "dos" and avoid the "don'ts," that, at four o'clock that first Monday, he won from the stern but would-be-just Farmer Holly his freedom for the rest of the day; and very gaily, he set off for a walk. He went without his violin as there was the smell of rain in the air, but his face and his step and the very swing of his arms were singing (to David) the joyous song of the morning before. Even yet, in spite of the vicissitudes of the day's work, the whole world, to David's homesick, lonely little heart, was still caroling that blessed "You're wanted, you're wanted, you're wanted!"

And then he saw the crow.

David knew crows. In his home on the mountain, he had had several of them for friends. He had learned to know and answer their calls. He had learned to admire their wisdom and to respect their moods and tempers. He loved to watch them. Especially he loved to see the great birds cut through the air with a wide sweep of wings, so alive, so gloriously free!

But this crow—

This crow was not cutting through the air with a wide sweep of its wings. It was in the middle of a cornfield, and it was rising and falling and flopping about in a most extraordinary fashion. Very soon David, running toward it, saw why. It was fastened securely, by a long leather strip, to a stake in the ground.

"Oh, oh, oh!" exclaimed David, in sympathetic consternation. "Here, you just wait a minute. I'll fix it."

With confidence, David whipped out his jackknife to cut the thong, but he found then that to "fix it" and to say he would "fix it" were two different matters.

The crow did not seem to recognize a friend in David. He saw in him, apparently, but another of the stone-throwing, gun-shooting, torturing humans who were responsible for his present hateful captivity. With beak and claw and wing, therefore, he fought this new evil that had come presumably to torment; and it wasn't until David had hit upon the expedient of taking off his blouse and throwing it over the angry bird that he could get near enough to accomplish his purpose. Even then David had to leave a twist of leather upon the slender leg.

A moment later, with a whir of wings and a frightened squawk that quickly turned into a surprised caw of triumphant rejoicing, the crow soared into the air and made straight for a distant treetop. David, after a minute's glad surveying of his work, donned his blouse again and resumed his walk.

It was almost six o'clock when David got back to the Holly farmhouse. In the barn doorway sat Perry Larson.

"Well, Sonny," the man greeted him cheerily, "did ye get yer weeding done?"

"Y—yes," hesitated David. "I got it done, but I didn't like it."

"It's kind of hot work."

"Oh, I didn't mind that part," returned David. "What I didn't like was pulling up all those pretty little plants and letting them die."

"Weeds—'pretty little plants'!" bellowed the man. "Well, I'll be jiggered!"

"But they were pretty," defended David, reading aright the scorn in Perry Larson's voice. "The very prettiest and biggest there were, always. Mr. Holly showed me, you know—and I had to pull them up."

"Well, I'll be jiggered!" muttered Perry Larson again.

"But I've been to walk since. I feel better now."

"Oh, ye do!"

"Oh, yes. I had a splendid walk. I went way up in the woods on the hill there. I was singing all the time—inside, you know. I was so glad Mrs. Holly wanted me. You know what it is, when you sing inside?"

Perry Larson scratched his head. "Well, no, sonny, I can't really say I do," he retorted. "I ain't much on singing."

"Oh, but I don't mean aloud. I mean inside. When you're happy, you know."

"When I'm—oh!" The man stopped and stared, his mouth

falling open. Suddenly his face changed, and he grinned appreciatively. "Well, if you ain't the beat 'em, boy! Tis kinder like singing'—the way ye feel inside when you're especially happy, ain't it? But I never thought of it before."

"Oh, yes. Why, that's where I get my songs—inside of me, you know—that I play on my violin. And I made a crow sing, too. Only he sang outside."

"Sing? A crow!" scoffed the man. "It'll take more 'n you to make me think a crow can sing, my lad."

"But they do, when they're happy," maintained the boy. "Anyhow, it doesn't sound the same as it does when they're cross or plagued over something. You ought to have heard this one today. He sang. He was so glad to get away. I let him loose, you see."

"You mean, you caught a crow up there in them woods?" The man's voice was skeptical.

"Oh, no, I didn't catch it. But somebody had, and tied him up. And he was so unhappy!"

"A crow tied up in the woods!"

"Oh, I didn't find it in the woods. It was before I went up the hill at all."

"A crow tied up—Look a-here, boy, what are you talking about? Where was that crow?" Perry Larson's whole self had become suddenly alert.

"In the field way over there. And somebody—"

"The cornfield! Jingo! Boy, you don't mean you touched that crow?"

"Well, he wouldn't let me touch him," half-apologized David. "He was so afraid, you see. Why, I had to put my blouse over his head before he'd let me cut him loose at all."

"Cut him loose!" Perry Larson sprang to his feet. "You didn't— you didn't let that crow go!"

David shrank back.

"Why, yes. He wanted to go. He—" But the man before him had fallen back despairingly to his old position.

"Well, sir, you've done it now. What the boss'll say, I don't know, but I know what I'd like to say to you. I was a whole week, off and on, getting hold of that crow, and I wouldn't have got him at all if I hadn't hid half the night and all the mornin' in that clump o' bushes, watchin' a chance to wing him, jest enough and not too much. And even then the job wasn't done. Let me tell you, 'twasn't no small thing to get him hitched. I'm wearin' the marks of the rascal's beak yet. And now you've gone and let him go—just like that," he finished, snapping his fingers angrily.

In David's face there was no contrition. There was only incredulous horror.

"You mean, you tied him there, on purpose?"

"Sure I did!"

"But he didn't like it. Couldn't you see he didn't like it?" cried David.

"Like it! What if he didn't? I didn't like to have my corn pulled up, either. See here, sonny, you no need to talk at me in that tone o' voice. I didn't hurt the varmint none to speak of—ye see he could fly, didn't ye?—and he wasn't starvin'. I saw to it that he had enough to eat and a dish o' water handy. And if he didn't flop and pull and try to get away, he needn't 'a' hurt hisself never. I ain't to blame for what pulling he done."

"But wouldn't you pull if you had two big wings that could carry you to the top of that big tree there, and away up, up in the sky where you could talk to the stars? Wouldn't you pull if somebody a hundred times bigger'n you came along and tied your leg to that post there?"

The man, Perry, flushed an angry red. "See here, sonny, I wasn't asking you to do no preachin'. What I did ain't no more'n any man 'round here does—if he's smart enough to catch one. Rigged-up broomsticks ain't in it with a live bird when it comes to drivin' away them pesky, thieving crows. There ain't a farmer 'round here that hain't been green with envy, ever since I caught the critter. And now to have you come along and with one flip of your knife spoil it all, I—Well, it jest makes me mad, clean through! That's all."

"You mean, you tied him there to frighten away the other crows?"

"Sure! There ain't nothing like it."

"Oh, I'm so sorry!"

"Well, you'd better be. But that won't bring back my crow!"

David's face brightened.

"No, that's so, isn't it? I'm glad of that. I was thinking of the crows, you see. I'm so sorry for them! Only think how we'd hate to be tied like that—" But Perry Larson, with a stare and an indignant snort, had gotten to his feet and was rapidly walking toward the house.

Very plainly David was in disgrace that evening, and it took all of Mrs. Holly's tact and patience, and some private pleading, to keep a general explosion from wrecking all chances of his staying any longer at the farmhouse. Even as it was, David was sorrowfully aware that he was proving to be a great disappointment so soon, and his violin playing that evening carried a moaning plaintiveness that would have been very significant to one who knew David well.

Very faithfully, the next day, the boy tried to carry out all the "dos," and though he did not always succeed, yet his efforts were so obvious that even the indignant owner of the liberated crow was somewhat mollified; and again Simeon Holly released David from work at four o'clock.

Alas, for David's peace of mind, however. For on his walk today, though he found no captive crow to demand his sympathy, he found something else quite as heartrending and as incomprehensible.

It was on the edge of the woods that he came upon two boys, each carrying a rifle, a dead squirrel, and a dead rabbit. The threatened rain of the day before had not materialized, and David had his violin. He had been playing softly when he came upon the boys where the path entered the woods.

"Oh!" At sight of the boys and their burden David gave an involuntary cry, and stopped playing.

The boys, scarcely less surprised to see David and his violin, paused and stared frankly.

"It's the tramp kid with his fiddle," whispered one to the other huskily.

David, his grieved eyes on the motionless little bodies in the boys' hands, shuddered.

"Are they—dead, too?"

The bigger boy nodded self-importantly.

"Sure. We just shot it—the squirrel. Ben here trapped the rabbit." He paused, manifestly waiting for the proper awed admiration to come into David's face.

But in David's startled eyes there was no awed admiration, there was only disbelieving horror.

"You mean, you *sent* them to the far country?"

"We—what?"

"Sent them. Made them go yourselves—to the far country?"

The younger boy still stared. The older one grinned disagreeably.

"Sure," he answered with laconic indifference. "We sent 'em to the far country, all right."

"But—how did you know they wanted to go?"

"Wanted— Eh?" exploded the big boy. Then he grinned again, still more disagreeably. "Well, you see, my dear, we didn't ask 'em," he gibed.

Real distress came into David's face.

"Then you don't know at all. And maybe they didn't want to go. And if they didn't, how could they go singing, as Father said? Father wasn't sent. He went. And he went singing. He said he did. But these—how would you like to have somebody come along and send you to the far country without even knowing if you wanted to go?"

There was no answer. The boys, with a growing fear in their eyes, as at sight of something inexplicable and uncanny, were sidling away; and in a moment they were hurrying down the hill, not, however, without a backward glance or two, of something very like terror.

David, left alone, went on his way with troubled eyes and a thoughtful frown.

David often wore, during those first few days at the Holly farmhouse, a thoughtful face and a troubled frown. There were so many, many things that were different from his mountain home. Over and over, as those first long days passed, he read his letter until he knew it by heart—and he had need to. Was he not already surrounded by things and people that were strange to him?

And they were so very strange—these people! There were the boys and men who rose at dawn—yet never paused to watch the sun flood the world with light; who stayed in the fields all day— yet never raised their eyes to the big fleecy clouds overhead; who knew birds only as thieves after fruit and grain, and squirrels and rabbits only as creatures to be trapped or shot. The women—they were even more incomprehensible. They spent the long hours behind screened doors and windows, washing the same dishes and sweeping the same floors day after day. They, too, never raised their eyes to the blue sky outside, nor even to the crimson roses that peeped in at the window. They seemed rather to be looking always for dirt, yet not pleased when they found it—especially if it had been tracked in on the heel of a small boy's shoe!

More extraordinary than all this to David, however, was the fact that these people regarded him, not themselves, as being strange. As if it were not the most natural thing in the world to live with one's father in one's home on the mountaintop, and spend one's days trailing through the forest paths or lying with a book beside some babbling little stream! As if it were not equally natural to take one's violin with one at times and learn to catch upon the quivering strings the whisper of the winds through the trees! Even in winter, when the clouds themselves came down from the sky and covered the earth with their soft whiteness—even then the forest was beautiful; and the song of the brook under its icy coat carried a charm and mystery that were quite wanting in the chattering freedom of summer. Surely there was nothing strange in all this, and yet these people seemed to think there was!

CHAPTER 9

Joe

D AY BY DAY, HOWEVER, AS TIME PASSED, DAVID DILIGENTLY tried to perform the "dos" and avoid the "don'ts;" and day by day he came to realize how important weeds and wood boxes were, if he were to conform to what was evidently Farmer Holly's idea of "playing in tune" in this strange new Orchestra of Life in which he found himself.

But, try as he would, there was yet an unreality about it all, a persistent feeling of uselessness and waste that would not be set aside. So that, after all, the only part of this strange new life of his that seemed real to him was the time that came after four o'clock each day when he was released from work.

And how full he filled those hours! There was so much to see, so much to do. For sunny days, there were fields and streams and pasture lands and the whole wide town to explore. For rainy days, if he did not care to go on a walk, there was his room with the books in the chimney cupboard. Some of them David had read before, but many of them he had not. One or two were old friends, but not so *Daredevil Dick*, and *The Pirates of Pigeon Cove* (which he found hidden in an obscure corner behind a loose board). Side by side stood *The Lady of the Lake*, *Treasure Island*, and *David Copperfield*; and coverless and dogeared lay *Robinson Crusoe*, and *The Arabian Nights*. There were more, many more, and David devoured them all with eager eyes. The good in them he absorbed as he absorbed the sunshine; the evil he cast aside unconsciously. It rolled off, indeed, like the proverbial water from the duck's back.

David hardly knew sometimes which he liked the better, his imaginative adventures between the covers of his books or his real adventures in his daily strolls. True, it was not his mountain home—this place in which he found himself; neither was his Silver Lake anywhere with its far, far-reaching sky above. More deplorable yet, nowhere was there the dear father he loved so well. But the sun still set in rose and gold, and the sky, though small, still carried the snowy sails of its cloud boats; while as to his father—his father had told him not to grieve, and David was trying very hard to obey.

David started out each day with his violin for company, unless he elected to stay indoors with his books. Sometimes it was toward the village that he turned his steps; sometimes it was toward the hills in back of the town. Whichever way it was, there was always sure to be something waiting at the end for him and his violin to discover, even if it was nothing more than a big white rose in bloom or a squirrel sitting by the roadside.

Very soon, however, David discovered that there was something to be found in his wanderings besides squirrels and roses—and that was people. In spite of the strangeness of these people, they were wonderfully interesting, David thought. And after that, he turned his steps more and more frequently toward the village when four o'clock released him from the day's work.

At first David did not talk much to these people. He shrank sensitively from their bold stares and unpleasantly audible comments. He watched them with round eyes of wonder and interest, however, when he did not think they were watching him. And in time, he came to know a lot about them and about the strange ways in which they passed their time.

There was the greenhouse man. It would be pleasant to spend

one's day growing plants and flowers—but not under that hot, stifling glass roof, decided David. Besides, he would not want always to pick and send away the very prettiest ones to the city every morning, as the greenhouse man did.

There was the doctor who rode all day long behind the gray mare, making sick folks well. David liked him, and mentally vowed that he himself would be a doctor sometime. Still, there was the stage-driver—David was not sure but he would prefer to follow this man's profession for a life work; for in his, one could still have the freedom of long days in the open, and yet not be saddened by the sight of the sick before they had been made well—which was where the stage driver had the better of the doctor, in David's opinion. There were the blacksmith and the storekeepers, too, but to these David gave little thought or attention.

Though he might not know what he did want to do, he knew very well what he did not. All of which merely goes to prove that David was still on the lookout for that great work which his father had said was waiting for him out in the world.

Meanwhile, David played his violin. If he found a crimson rambler in bloom in a dooryard, he put it into a little melody of pure delight—that a woman in the house behind the rambler heard the music and was cheered at her task, David did not know. If he found a kitten at play in the sunshine, he put it into a riotous abandonment of tumbling turns and trills—that a fretful baby heard and stopped its wailing, David also did not know. And once, just because the sky was blue and the air was sweet, and it was so good to be alive, David lifted his bow and put it all into a rapturous paean of ringing exultation—that a sick man in a darkened chamber above the street lifted his head, drew in his breath, and took suddenly a new lease on life, David still again did not know. All of which merely goes to prove that David had perhaps found his work and was doing it—although, yet still again, David did not know.

It was in the cemetery one afternoon that David came upon the Lady in Black. She was on her knees putting flowers on a little mound before her. She looked up as David approached. For a moment she gazed wistfully at him; then, as if impelled by a hidden force, she spoke.

"Little boy, who are you?"

"I'm David."

"David! David who? Do you live here? I've seen you here before."

"Oh, yes, I've been here quite a lot of times." Purposely the boy evaded the questions. David was getting tired of questions—especially these questions.

"And have you—lost someone dear to you, little boy?"

"Lost someone?"

"I mean—is your father or mother—here?"

"Here? Oh, no, they aren't here. My mother is an angel mother, and my father has gone to the far country. He is waiting for me there, you know."

"But, that's the same—That is—" She stopped helplessly, bewildered eyes on David's serene face. Then suddenly a great light came to her own. "Oh, little boy, I wish I could understand that—just that," she breathed. "It would make it so much easier if I could just remember that they aren't here—that they're waiting—over there!"

But David apparently did not hear. He had turned and was playing softly as he walked away. Silently the Lady in Black knelt, listening, looking after him. When she rose some time later and left the cemetery, the light in her face was still there, deeper, more glorified.

Toward boys and girls—especially boys—of his own age, David frequently turned wistful eyes. David wanted a friend, a friend who would know and understand, a friend who would see things as he saw them, who would understand what he was saying when he played. It seemed to David that he ought to find such a friend in some boy of his own age. He had seen many boys, but he had not yet found the friend. David had begun to think, indeed, that, of all these strange beings in this new life of his, boys were the strangest.

They stared and nudged each other unpleasantly when they came upon him playing. They jeered when he tried to tell them what he had been playing. They had never heard of the great Orchestra of Life, and they fell into most disconcerting fits of laughter, or else backed away as if afraid, when he told them that they themselves were instruments in it, and that if they did not keep themselves in tune, there was sure to be a discord somewhere.

Then there were their games and frolics. Those that were played with balls, bats, and bags of beans, David thought he would like very much to play. But the boys only scoffed when he asked them to teach him how to play. They laughed when a dog chased a cat, and they thought it very, very funny when Tony, the old black man, tripped on the string they drew across his path. They liked to throw stones and shoot guns, and the more creeping, crawling, or flying creatures that they could send to the far country, the happier they were, apparently. Nor did they like it at all when he asked them if they were sure all these creeping, crawling, flying creatures wanted to leave this beautiful world and to be made dead. They sneered and called him a sissy. David did not know what a sissy was, but from the way they said it, he judged it must be even worse to be a sissy than to be a thief.

And then he discovered Joe.

David had found himself in a very strange, very unlovely neighborhood that afternoon. The street was full of papers and tin cans; the houses were unspeakably forlorn with sagging blinds and lack of paint. Untidy women and bleary-eyed men leaned over the dilapidated fences or lolled on mud-tracked doorsteps. David, his shrinking eyes turning from one side to the other, passed slowly through the street, his violin under his arm. Nowhere could David find here the tiniest spot of beauty to "play." He had reached quite the most forlorn little shanty on the street when the promise in his father's letter occurred to him. With a suddenly illumined face, he raised his violin to position and plunged into a veritable whirl of trills and runs and tripping melodies.

"If I didn't just entirely forget that I didn't need to see anything beautiful to play," laughed David softly to himself. "Why, it's already right here in my violin!"

David had passed the tumble-down shanty and was hesitating where two streets crossed, when he felt a light touch on his arm. He turned to confront a small girl in a patched and faded calico dress, obviously outgrown. Her eyes were wide and frightened. In the middle of her outstretched dirty little palm was a copper cent.

"If you please, Joe sent this—to you," she faltered.

"To me? What for?" David stopped playing and lowered his violin.

The little girl backed away perceptibly, though she still held out the coin. "He wanted you to stay and play some more. He said to tell you he'd have sent more money if he could. But he didn't have it. He just had this cent."

David's eyes flew wide open.

"You mean he wants me to play? He likes it?" he asked joyfully.

"Yes. He said he knew 't wasn't much—the cent. But he thought maybe you'd play a little for it."

"Play? Of course I'll play" cried David. "Oh, no, I don't want the money," he added, waving the again-proffered coin aside. "I don't need money where I'm living now. Where is he—the one that wants me to play?" he finished eagerly.

"In there by the window. It's Joe. He's my brother." The little girl, in spite of her evident satisfaction at the accomplishment of her purpose, kept quite aloof from the boy. Nor did the fact that he refused the money appear to bring her anything but uneasy surprise.

In the window David saw a boy apparently about his own age, a boy with sandy hair, pale cheeks, and wide-open, curiously intent blue eyes.

"Is he coming? Did you get him? Will he play?" called the boy at the window eagerly.

"Yes, I'm right here. I'm the one. Can't you see the violin? Shall I play here or come in?" answered David, not one whit less eagerly.

The small girl opened her lips as if to explain something, but the boy in the window did not wait. "Oh, come in. Will you come in?" he cried unbelievingly. "And will you just let me touch it—the fiddle? Come! You will come? See, there isn't anybody home, only just Betty and me."

"Of course I will!" David fairly stumbled up the broken steps in his impatience to reach the wide-open door. "Did you like it— what I played? And did you know what I was playing? Did you understand? Could you see the cloud-boats up in the sky and my Silver Lake down in the valley? And could you hear the birds, and the winds in the trees, and the little brooks? Could you? Oh, did you understand? I've so wanted to find someone that could! But I wouldn't think that you—here—" With a gesture, and an expression on his face that was unmistakable, David came to a helpless pause.

"There, Joe, what'd I tell you," cried the little girl, in a husky whisper, darting to her brother's side. "Oh, why did you make me get him here? Everybody says he's crazy as a loon, and—"

But the boy reached out a quickly silencing hand. His face was curiously alight, as if from an inward glow. His eyes, still widely intent, were staring straight ahead.

"Stop, Betty, wait," he hushed her. "Maybe—I think I do understand. Boy, you mean—inside of you, you see those things, and then you try to make your fiddle tell what you are seeing. Is that it?"

"Yes, yes," cried David. "Oh, you do understand. And I never thought you could. I never thought that anybody could that didn't have anything to look at but him—but these things."

"'Anything but these things to look at'!" echoed the boy, with a sudden anguish in his voice. "Anything but these things! I guess if I could see anything, I wouldn't mind what I see! and you wouldn't, neither, if you were—blind, like me."

"Blind!" David fell back. Face and voice were full of horror. "You mean you can't see anything with your eyes?"

"Nothing."

"Oh! I never saw anyone blind before. There was one in a book—but Father took it away. Since then, in books down here, I've found others, but—"

"Yes, yes. Well, never mind that," cut in the blind boy, growing restive under the pity in the other's voice. "Play, won't you?"

"But how are you ever going to know what a beautiful world it is?" shuddered David. "How can you know? And how can you ever play in tune? You're one of the instruments. Father said everybody was. And he said everybody was playing something all the time, and if you didn't play in tune—"

"Joe, Joe, please," begged the little girl, "won't you let him go? I'm afraid. I told you—"

"He won't hurt ye, Betty," laughed Joe, a little irritably. Then to David he turned again with some sharpness. "Play, won't ye? You said you'd play!"

"Yes, oh, yes, I'll play," faltered David, bringing his violin hastily to position, and then testing the strings with fingers that shook a little.

"There!" breathed Joe, settling back in his chair with a contented sigh. "Now, play it again—what you did before."

But David did not play what he did before—at first. There were no airy cloud-boats, no far-reaching sky, no birds or murmuring forest brooks in his music this time. There were only the poverty-stricken room, the dirty street, the boy alone at the window with his sightless eyes—the boy who never, never would know what a beautiful world he lived in.

Then suddenly to David came a new thought. This boy, Joe, had said before that he understood. He had seemed to know that he was being told of the sunny skies and the forest winds, the singing birds and the babbling brooks. Perhaps again now he would understand.

What if, for those sightless eyes, one could create a world?

Possibly never before had David played as he played then. It was as if upon those four quivering strings, he was laying the purple and gold of a thousand sunsets, the rose and amber of a thousand sunrises, the green of a boundless earth, the blue of a sky that reached to heaven itself—to make Joe understand.

"Gee!" breathed Joe, when the music came to an end with a crashing chord. "Say, wasn't that just great? Won't you let me, please, just touch that fiddle?" And David, looking into the blind boy's exalted face, knew that Joe had indeed understood.

CHAPTER 10

The Lady of the Roses

IT WAS A NEW WORLD, INDEED, THAT DAVID CREATED FOR JOE after that, a world that had to do with entrancing music where once was silence, delightful companionship where once was loneliness, and toothsome cookies and doughnuts where once was hunger.

The Widow Glaspell, Joe's mother, worked out by the day, scrubbing and washing; and Joe, perforce, was left to the somewhat erratic and decidedly unskillful ministrations of Betty. Betty was no worse, and no better, than any other untaught, irresponsible twelve-year-old girl, and it was not to be expected, perhaps, that she would care to spend all the bright sunny hours shut up with her sorely afflicted and somewhat fretful brother. True, at noon she never failed to appear and prepare something that passed for a dinner for herself and Joe. But the Glaspell larder was frequently almost as empty as were the hungry stomachs that looked to it for refreshment; and it would have taken a far more skillful cook than was the fly-away Betty to evolve anything from it that was either palatable or satisfying.

With David coming into Joe's life, all this was changed. First, there were the music and the companionship. Joe's father had "played in the band" in his youth, and (according to the Widow Glaspell) had been a "powerful hand for music." It was from him, presumably, that Joe had inherited his passion for melody and harmony; and it was no wonder that David recognized so soon in the blind boy the spirit that made them kin. At the first stroke of David's bow, indeed, the dingy walls about them would crumble into nothingness, and together the two boys were off in a world of loveliness and joy.

Nor was listening always Joe's part. From "just touching" the violin—his first longing plea—he came to drawing a timid bow across the strings. In an incredibly short time, then, he was picking out bits of melody; and by the end of a fortnight, David had brought his father's violin for Joe to practice on.

"I can't give it to you, not for keeps," David had explained, a bit tremulously, "because it was Daddy's, you know; and when I see it, it seems almost as if I were seeing him. But you may take it. Then you can have it here to play on whenever you like."

After that, in Joe's own hands lay the power to transport himself into another world, for with the violin for company, he knew no loneliness.

Nor was the violin all that David brought to the house. There were the doughnuts and the cookies. David had discovered very early in his visits, and much to his surprise, that Joe and Betty were often hungry.

"But why don't you go down to the store and buy something?" he had queried at once.

Upon being told that there was no money to buy with, David's first impulse had been to bring several of the gold pieces the next time he came; but upon second thoughts, David decided that he did not dare. He was not wishing to be called a thief a second time. It would be better, he concluded, to bring some food from the house instead.

In his mountain home, everything the house afforded in the way of food had always been freely given to the few strangers that found their way to the cabin door. So now David had no hesitation in going to Mrs. Holly's pantry for supplies, upon the occasion of his next visit to Joe Glaspell's.

Mrs. Holly, coming into the kitchen, found him emerging from the pantry with both hands full of cookies and doughnuts.

"Why, David, what in the world does this mean?" she demanded.

"They're for Joe and Betty," smiled David happily.

"For Joe and— But those doughnuts and cookies don't belong to you. They're mine!"

"Yes, I know they are. I told them you had plenty," nodded David.

"Plenty! What if I have?" remonstrated Mrs. Holly, in growing indignation. "That doesn't mean that you can take—" Something in David's face stopped the words half-spoken.

"You don't mean that I can't take them to Joe and Betty, do you? Why, Mrs. Holly, they're hungry! Joe and Betty are. They don't have half enough to eat. Betty said so. And we've got more than we want. There's food left on the table every day. Why, if *you* were hungry, wouldn't you want somebody to bring—"

But Mrs. Holly stopped him with a despairing gesture.

"There, there, never mind. Run along. Of course you can take them. I'm—I'm glad to have you," she finished, in a desperate attempt to drive from David's face that look of shocked incredulity with which he was still regarding her.

Never again did Mrs. Holly attempt to thwart David's generosity to the Glaspells, but she did try to regulate it. She saw to it that, thereafter upon his visits to the house, he took only certain things and a certain amount, and invariably things of her own choosing.

But not always toward the Glaspell's shanty did David turn his steps. Very frequently it was in quite another direction. He had been at the Holly farmhouse three weeks when he found his Lady of the Roses.

He had passed quite through the village that day and had
come to a road that was new to him. It was a beautiful road,
smooth, white, and firm. Two huge granite posts topped with
flaming nasturtiums marked the point where it turned off from
the main highway. Beyond these, as David soon found, it ran
between wide-spreading lawns and flowering shrubs, leading up
the gentle slope of a hill. Where it led to David did not know, but
he proceeded unhesitatingly to try to find out. For some time he
climbed the slope in silence, his violin mute under his arm, but
the white road still lay in tantalizing mystery before him when a
by-path offered the greater temptation and lured him to explore its
cool shadowy depths instead.

Had David but known it, he was at Sunnycrest, Hinsdale's one
"show place," the country home of its one really rich resident, Miss
Barbara Holbrook. Had he also but known it, Miss Holbrook was
not celebrated for her graciousness to any visitors, certainly not to
those who ventured to approach her otherwise than by a conven-
tional ring at her front doorbell. But David did not know all this,
and he, therefore, very happily followed the shady path until he
came to the Wonder at the end of it.

The Wonder, in Hinsdale parlance, was only Miss Holbrook's
garden, but in David's eyes it was incredible. For one whole minute
he could only stand like a very ordinary little boy and stare. At
the end of the minute, he became himself once more, and being
himself, he expressed his delight at once in the only way he knew
how—by raising his violin and beginning to play.

He had meant to tell of the limpid pool and of the arch of the
bridge it reflected; of the terraced lawns and marble steps, and of
the gleaming white of the sculptured nymphs and fauns; of the
splashes of glorious crimson, yellow, blush-pink, and snowy white
against the green, where the roses rioted in luxurious bloom.
He had meant, also, to tell of the Queen Rose of them all—the

beauteous lady with hair like the gold of sunrise and a gown like the shimmer of the moon on water—of all this he had meant to tell, but he had scarcely begun to tell it at all when the Beauteous Lady of the Roses sprang to her feet and became so very much like an angry young woman who is seriously displeased that David could only lower his violin in dismay.

"Why, boy, what does this mean?" she demanded.

David sighed a little impatiently as he came forward into the sunlight.

"But I was just telling you," he remonstrated, "and you would not let me finish."

"Telling me!"

"Yes, with my violin. Couldn't you understand?" appealed the boy wistfully. "You looked as if you could!"

"Looked as if I could!"

"Yes. Joe understood, you see, and I was surprised when he did. But I was just sure you could—with all this to look at."

The lady frowned. Half-unconsciously she glanced about her as if contemplating flight. Then she turned back to the boy.

"But how came you here? Who are you?" she asked.

"I'm David. I walked here through the little path back there. I didn't know where it went to, but I'm so glad now I found out!"

"Oh, are you!" murmured the lady, with slightly uplifted brows.

She was about to tell him very coldly that now that he had found his way there he might occupy himself in finding it home again, when the boy interposed rapturously, his eyes sweeping the scene before him. "Yes. I didn't suppose that anywhere down here there was a place one half so beautiful!"

An odd feeling of uncanniness sent a swift exclamation to the lady's lips. "'Down here'! What do you mean by that? You speak as if you came from—above," she almost laughed.

"I did," returned David simply. "But even up there, I never

found anything quite like this—" With a sweep of his hands, he finished with an admiration that was as open as it was ardent. "—nor like you, O Lady of the Roses."

This time the lady laughed outright. She even blushed a little.

"Very prettily put, Sir Flatterer," she retorted. "But when you are older, young man, you won't make your compliments quite so broad. I am no Lady of the Roses. I am Miss Holbrook, and—and I am not in the habit of receiving gentlemen callers who are uninvited and unannounced," she concluded, a little sharply.

Pointless, the shaft fell at David's feet. He had turned again to the beauties about him, and at that moment he spied the sundial—something he had never seen before.

"What is it?" he cried eagerly, hurrying forward. "It isn't exactly pretty, and yet it looks as if it were meant for—something."

"It is. It is a sundial. It marks the time by the sun."

Even as she spoke, Miss Holbrook wondered why she answered the question at all, and why she did not send this small piece of nonchalant impertinence about his business, as he so richly deserved. The next instant, she found herself staring at the boy in amazement. With unmistakable ease, and with the trained accent of the scholar, he was reading aloud the Latin inscription on the dial: "'Horas non numero nisi serenas.' I count—no—hours but—unclouded ones," he then translated slowly, though with confidence. "That's pretty; but what does it mean—about 'counting'?"

Miss Holbrook rose to her feet. "Goodness, boy, who and what are you?" she demanded. "Can you read Latin?"

"Why, of course! Can't you?"

With a disdainful gesture, Miss Holbrook swept this aside. "Boy, who are you?" she demanded again imperatively.

"I'm David. I told you."

"But David who? Where do you live?"

The boy's face clouded. "I'm David—just David. I live at Farmer

Holly's now, but I did live on the mountain with—Father, you know."

A great light of understanding broke over Miss Holbrook's face. She dropped back into her seat. "Oh, I remember," she murmured. "You're the little—er—boy whom he took in. I have heard the story. So that is who you are," she added, the old look of aversion coming back to her eyes. She had almost said "the little tramp boy," but she had stopped in time.

"Yes. And now what do they mean, please—those words—'I count no hours but unclouded ones'?"

Miss Holbrook stirred in her seat and frowned. "Why, it means what it says, of course, boy. A sundial counts its hours by the shadow the sun throws, and when there is no sun there is no shadow; hence, it's only the sunny hours that are counted by the dial," she explained a little fretfully.

David's face radiated delight.

"Oh, but I like that!" he exclaimed.

"You like it?"

"Yes. I should like to be one myself, you know."

"Well, really! And how, pray tell?" In spite of herself, a faint gleam of interest came into Miss Holbrook's eyes.

David laughed and dropped himself easily to the ground at her feet. He was holding his violin on his knees now. "Why, it would be such fun," he chuckled, "to just forget all about the hours when the sun didn't shine and remember only the nice, pleasant ones. Now for me, there wouldn't be any hours, really, until after four o'clock, except little specks of minutes that I'd get in between when I did see something interesting."

Miss Holbrook stared frankly. "What an extraordinary boy you are, to be sure," she murmured. "And what, may I ask, is it that you do every day until four o'clock that you wish to forget?"

David sighed. "Well, there are lots of things. I hoed potatoes and corn, first, but they're too big now, mostly; and I pulled up weeds, too, till they were gone. I've been picking up stones, lately, and clearing up the yard. Then, of course, there's always the wood box to fill, and the eggs to hunt, besides the chickens to feed— though I don't mind them so much, but I do the other things, 'specially the weeds. They were so much prettier than the things I had to let grow, 'most always."

Miss Holbrook laughed.

"Well, they were, and really," persisted the boy, in answer to the merriment in her eyes. "Now wouldn't it be nice to be like the sundial and forget everything the sun didn't shine on? Wouldn't you like it? Isn't there anything you want to forget?"

Miss Holbrook sobered instantly. The change in her face was so very marked, indeed, that involuntarily David looked about for something that might have cast upon it so great a shadow. For a long minute she did not speak; then very slowly, very bitterly, she said aloud, yet as if to herself, "Yes. If I had my way, I'd forget them every one—these hours, every single one!"

"Oh, Lady of the Roses!" expostulated David in a voice quivering with shocked dismay. "You don't mean—you can't mean that you don't have any sun!"

"I mean just that," bowed Miss Holbrook wearily, her eyes on the somber shadows of the pool, "just that!"

David sat stunned, confounded. The shadows lengthened across the marble steps and the terraces, and David watched them as the sun dipped behind the treetops. They seemed to make more vivid the chill and the gloom of the lady's words—more real her day that had no sun. After a time, the boy picked up his violin and began to play softly, and, at first, with evident hesitation. Even when his touch became more confident, there was still in the music a questioning appeal that seemed to find no answer, an appeal that even the player himself could not have explained.

For many long minutes the young woman and the boy sat thus in the twilight. Then suddenly the woman got to her feet. "Come, come, boy, what can I be thinking of?" she cried sharply. "I must go in, and you must go home. Goodnight." And she swept across the grass to the path that led toward the house.

CHAPTER 11

Jack and Jill

D AVID WAS TEMPTED TO GO FOR A SECOND VISIT TO his Lady of the Roses, but something he could not define held him back. The lady was in his mind almost constantly, however; and the picture of the garden was very vivid to him, though it was always as he had seen it last—with the hush and shadow of twilight, and with the lady's face gloomily turned toward the sunless pool. David could not forget that, for her, there were no hours to count; she had said it herself. He could not understand how this could be so, and the thought filled him with vague unrest and pain.

Perhaps it was this restlessness that drove David to explore the village itself even more persistently, sending him into new streets in search of something strange and interesting. One day the sound of shouts and laughter drew him to an open lot in back of the church where some boys were at play.

David still knew very little about boys. In his mountain home, he had never had them for playmates, and he had not seen much of them when he went with his father to the mountain village for supplies. There had been, it is true, the boy who frequently brought milk and eggs to the cabin, but he had been very quiet and shy, appearing always afraid and anxious to get away, as if he had been told not to stay. More recently, since David had been at the Holly farmhouse, his experience with

boys had been even less satisfying. The boys—with the exception
of blind Joe—had very clearly let it be understood that they had
little use for a youth who could find nothing better to do than to
tramp through the woods and the streets with a fiddle under his
arm.

Today, however, there came a change. Perhaps they were more
used to him, or perhaps they had decided suddenly that it might
be good fun to satisfy their curiosity, anyway, regardless of conse-
quences. Whatever it was, the lads hailed his appearance with wild
shouts of glee.

"Look, boys! Here's the fiddlin' kid," yelled one, and the others
joined in the "Hurrah!" he gave.

David smiled delightedly. Once more he had found someone
who wanted him, and it was so nice to be wanted! Truth to tell,
David had felt not a little hurt at the persistent avoidance of all
those boys and girls of his own age.

"How—how do you do?" he said diffidently, but still with that
beaming smile.

Again the boys shouted gleefully as they hurried forward.
Several had short sticks in their hands. One had an old tomato can
with a string tied to it. The tallest boy had something that he was
trying to hold beneath his coat.

"'H—how do you do?'" they mimicked. "How do you do,
fiddlin' kid?"

"I'm David; my name is David." The reminder was graciously
given, with a smile.

"David! David! His name is David," chanted the boys, as if they
were a comic-opera chorus.

David laughed outright. "Oh, sing it again, sing it again!" he
crowed. "That sounded fine!"

The boys stared, then sniffed disdainfully, and cast derisive
glances into each other's eyes. It appeared that this little sissy

tramp boy did not even know enough to discover when he was being laughed at!

"David! David! His name is David," they jeered into his face again. "Come on, tune her up! We want to dance."

"Play? Of course I'll play," cried David joyously, raising his violin and testing a string for its tone.

"Here, hold on," yelled the tallest boy. "The Queen o' the Ballet ain't ready." And he cautiously pulled from beneath his coat a struggling kitten with a perforated bag tied over its head.

"Sure! We want her in the middle," grinned the boy with the tin can. "Hold on till I get her train tied to her," he finished, trying to capture the swishing, fluffy tail of the frightened little cat.

David had begun to play, but he stopped his music with a discordant stroke of the bow.

"What are you doing? What is the matter with that cat?" he demanded.

"'Matter'!" called a derisive voice. "Sure, nothings the matter with her. She's the Queen o' the Ballet—she is!"

"What do you mean?" cried David. At that moment, the string bit hard into the captured tail, and the kitten cried out with the pain. "Look out! You're hurting her," cautioned David sharply.

Only a laugh and a jeering word answered. Then the kitten, with the bag on its head and the tin can tied to its tail, was let warily to the ground, the tall boy still holding its back with both hands.

"Ready, now! Come on, play," he ordered. "Then we'll set her dancing."

David's eyes flashed. "I will not play—for that."

The boys stopped laughing suddenly. "Eh? What?" They could scarcely have been more surprised if the kitten itself had said the words.

"I say, I won't play. I can't play—unless you let that cat go."

"Hoity-toity! Won't ye hear that now?" laughed a mocking

voice. "And what if we say we won't let her go, eh?"

"Then I'll make you," vowed David, aflame with a newborn something that seemed to have sprung full-grown into being.

"Yow!" hooted the tallest boy, removing both hands from the captive kitten.

The kitten, released, began to back up frantically. The can, dangling at its heels, rattled and banged and thumped until the frightened little creature, crazed with terror, became nothing but a whirling mass of misery. The boys, formed now into a crowing circle of delight, kept the kitten within bounds, and flouted David mercilessly.

"Ah, ha! Stop us, will ye? Why don't ye stop us?" they gibed.

For a moment David stood without movement, his eyes staring. The next instant, he turned and ran. The jeers became a chorus of triumphant shouts then—but not for long. David had only hurried to the woodpile to lay down his violin. He came back then, on the run; and before the tallest boy could catch his breath, he was felled by a stinging blow on the jaw.

Over by the church, a small girl, red-haired and red-eyed, clambered hastily over the fence behind which for long minutes she had been crying and wringing her hands.

"He'll be killed, he'll be killed," she moaned. "And it's my fault, 'cause it's my kitty—it's my kitty," she sobbed, straining her eyes to catch a glimpse of the kitten's protector in the squirming mass of legs and arms.

The kitten, unheeded now by the boys, was pursuing its backward whirl to destruction some distance away, and very soon the little girl discovered her. With a bound and a choking cry, she reached the kitten, removed the bag and unbound the cruel string. Then, sitting on the ground a safe distance away, she soothed the palpitating little bunch of gray fur and watched the fight with fearful eyes.

And what a fight it was! There was no question, of course, as to its final outcome, with six against one; but meanwhile, the one was giving the six the surprise of their lives in the shape of well-dealt blows and skillful twists and turns that caused their own strength and weight to react upon themselves in a most astonishing fashion. The one unmistakably was getting the worst of it, however, when the little girl, after a hurried dash to the street, brought back with her to the rescue a tall, smooth-shaven young man whom she had hailed from afar as "Jack."

Jack put a stop to things at once. With vigorous jerks and pulls, he unsnarled the writhing mass, boy by boy, each one of whom, upon catching sight of his face, slunk hurriedly away as if glad to escape so lightly. Finally, only David alone was left upon the ground. But when David did at last appear, the little girl burst into tears anew.

"Oh, Jack, he's killed—I know he's killed," she wailed. "And he was so nice and—and pretty. And now look at him! Ain't he a sight?"

David was not killed, but he was a sight. His blouse was torn, his tie was gone, and his face and hands were covered with dirt and blood. Above one eye was an ugly-looking lump, and below the other was a red bruise. Somewhat dazedly he responded to the man's helpful hand, pulled himself upright, and looked about him. He did not see the little girl behind him.

"Where's the cat?" he asked anxiously.

The unexpected happened then. With a sobbing cry, the little girl flung herself upon him, cat and all.

"Here, right here," she choked. "And it was you who saved her—my Juliette! And I'll love you, love you, love you always for it!"

"There, there, Jill," interposed the man a little hurriedly. "Suppose we first show our gratitude by seeing if we can't do something to make our young warrior here more comfortable."

And he began to brush off some of the accumulated dirt with his handkerchief.

"Why can't we take him home, Jack, and clean him up 'fore other folks see him?" suggested the girl.

The boy turned quickly. "Did you call him 'Jack'?"

"Yes."

"And he called you, Jill'?"

"Yes."

"The real 'Jack and Jill' that 'went up the hill'?"

The man and the girl laughed, but the girl shook her head as she answered, "Not really—though we do go up a hill, all right, every day. But those aren't even our own names. We just call each other that for fun. Don't *you* ever call things—for fun?"

David's face lighted up, in spite of the dirt, the lump, and the bruises. "Oh, do you do that?" he breathed. "Say, I just know I'd like to play to you! You'd understand!"

"Oh, yes, and he plays, too," explained the little girl, turning to the man rapturously. "On a fiddle, you know, like you."

She had not finished her sentence before David was away, hurrying a little unsteadily across the lot for his violin. When he came back, the man was looking at him with an anxious frown.

"Suppose you come home with us, boy," he said. "It isn't far— through the hill pasture, 'cross lots—and we'll look you over a bit. That lump over your eye needs attention."

"Thank you," beamed David. "I'd like to go, and—I'm glad you want me!" He spoke to the man, but he looked at the little red-headed girl, who still held the gray kitten in her arms.

CHAPTER 12

Answers That Do Not Answer

"JACK AND JILL," IT APPEARED, WERE A BROTHER AND SISTER who lived in a tiny house on a hill directly across the creek from Sunnycrest. Beyond this David learned little until after bumps and bruises and dirt had been carefully attended to. He had then, too, some questions to answer concerning himself.

"And now, if you please," began the man smilingly, as he surveyed the boy with an eye that could see no further service to be rendered, "do you mind telling me who you are, and how you came to be the center of attraction for the blows and cuffs of six boys?"

"I'm David, and I wanted the cat," returned the boy simply.

"Well, that's direct and to the point, to say the least," laughed the man. "Evidently, however, you're in the habit of being that. But David, there were six of them—those boys—and some of them were larger than you."

"Yes, sir."

"And they were so bad and cruel," chimed in the little girl.

The man hesitated, then questioned slowly. "And may I ask you where you—er—learned to—fight like that?"

"I used to box with Father. He said I must first be well and strong. He taught me jiujitsu, too, a little, but I couldn't make it work very well—with so many."

"I should say not," adjudged the man grimly. "But you gave

them a surprise or two, I'll warrant," he added. His eyes gazed on the cause of the trouble, now curled in a little gray bunch of contentment on the window sill. "But I don't know yet who you are. Who is your father? Where does he live?"

David shook his head. As was always the case when his father was mentioned, his face grew wistful and his eyes dreamy. "He doesn't live here anywhere," murmured the boy. "He is in the far country, waiting for me to come to him and tell him of the beautiful world I have found, you know."

"Eh? What?" stammered the man, not knowing whether to believe his eyes or his ears. This boy who fought like a demon and talked like a saint, and who, though battered and bruised, prattled of the "beautiful world" he had found, was most disconcerting.

"Why, Jack, don't you know?" whispered the little girl agitatedly. "He's the boy at Mr. Holly's that they took in." Then, still more softly, "He's the little tramp boy. His father died in the barn."

"Oh," said the man, his face clearing and his eyes showing a quick sympathy. "You're the boy at the Holly farmhouse, are you?"

"Yes, sir."

"And he plays the fiddle everywhere," volunteered the little girl, with ardent admiration. "If you hadn't been shut up sick just now, you'd have heard him yourself. He plays everywhere he goes."

"Is that so?" murmured Jack politely, shuddering a little at what he fancied would come from a violin played by a boy like the one before him. (Jack could play the violin himself a little—enough to know it some, and love it more.) "Hmm. Well, and what else do you do?"

"Nothing, except to go for walks and read."

"Nothing? A big boy like you—and on Simeon Holly's farm?" Voice and manner showed that Jack was not unacquainted with Simeon Holly and his methods and opinions.

David laughed gleefully. "Oh, of course, I do lots of things, only

I don't count those any more. 'Horas non numero nisi serenas,' you know," he quoted pleasantly, smiling into the man's astonished eyes.

"Jack, what was that—what did he say?" whispered the little girl. "It sounded foreign. Is he foreign?"

"You've got me, Jill," retorted the man, with a laughing grimace. "Heaven only knows what he is—I don't. What he said was Latin; I do happen to know that. Still—" He turned to the boy and said, ironically, "of course you know the translation of that."

"Oh, yes. 'I count no hours but unclouded ones.' And I liked that. It was on a sundial, you know; and *I'm* going to be a sundial and not count the hours I don't like—while I'm pulling up weeds, and hoeing potatoes, and picking up stones, and all that. Don't you see?"

For a moment, the man stared dumbly. Then he threw back his head and laughed. "Well, by George!" he muttered. "By George!" And he laughed again. Then, "And did your father teach you that, too?" he asked.

"Oh, no. Well, he taught me Latin, and so, of course, I could read it when I found it. But those special words I got off the sundial where my Lady of the Roses lives."

"Your Lady of the Roses! And who is she?"

"Why, don't you know? You live right in sight of her house," cried David, pointing to the towers of Sunnycrest that showed above the trees. "It's over there. I know those towers now, and I look for them wherever I go. I love them. It makes me see the roses all over again—and her."

"You mean—Miss Holbrook?"

The voice was so different from the genial tones that he had heard before that David looked up in surprise. "Yes, she said that was her name," he answered, wondering at the indefinable change that had come to the man's face.

There was a moment's pause, then the man rose to his feet. "How's your head? Does it ache?" he asked briskly.

"Not much—some. I—I think I'll be going," replied David a little awkwardly, reaching for his violin and unconsciously showing by his manner the sudden chill in the atmosphere.

The little girl spoke then. She overwhelmed him again with thanks and pointed to the contented kitten on the window sill. True, she did not tell him this time that she would love, love, love him always, but she beamed upon him gratefully, and she urged him to come again soon, and often.

David bowed himself off, with many a backward wave of the hand and many a promise to come again. Not until he had quite reached the bottom of the hill did he remember that the man, "Jack," had said almost nothing at the last. As David recollected him, indeed, he had last been seen standing beside one of the veranda posts, with gloomy eyes fixed on the towers of Sunnycrest that showed red-gold above the treetops in the last rays of the setting sun.

It was a bad half-hour that David spent at the Holly farmhouse in explanation of his torn blouse and bruised face. Farmer Holly did not approve of fights, and he said so, very sternly indeed. Even Mrs. Holly, who was usually so kind to him, let David understand that he was in deep disgrace, though she was very tender to his wounds.

David did venture to ask her, however, before he went upstairs to bed, "Mrs. Holly, who are those people—Jack and Jill—that were so good to me this afternoon?"

"They are John Gurnsey and his sister, Julia; but the whole town knows them by the names they long ago gave themselves, 'Jack' and 'Jill.'"

"And do they live all alone in the little house?"

"Yes, except for the Widow Glaspell, who comes in several

times a week, I believe, to cook and wash and sweep. They aren't very happy, I'm afraid, David, and I'm glad you could rescue the little girl's kitten for her. But you mustn't fight. No good can come of fighting!"

"I got the cat—by fighting."

"Yes, yes, I know, but—" She did not finish her sentence, and David was only waiting for a pause to ask another question.

"Why aren't they happy, Mrs. Holly?"

"Tut, tut, David, it's a long story, and you wouldn't understand it if I told it. It's only that they're all alone in the world, and Jack Gurnsey isn't well. He must be thirty years old now. He had bright hopes, not so long ago, of studying law, or something of the sort, in the city. Then his father died, and his mother, and he lost his health. Something ails his lungs, and the doctors sent him here to be outdoors. He even sleeps outdoors, they say. Anyway, he's here, and he's making a home for his sister; but, of course, with his hopes and ambitions—But there, David, you don't understand, of course!"

"Oh, yes, I do," breathed David, his eyes pensively turned toward a shadowy corner. "He found his work out in the world, and then he had to stop and couldn't do it. Poor Mr. Jack!"

CHAPTER 13

A Surprise for Mr. Jack

LIFE AT THE HOLLY FARMHOUSE WAS NOT WHAT IT HAD BEEN. The coming of David had introduced new elements that promised complications. Not because he was another mouth to feed—Simeon Holly was not worrying about that part any longer. Crops showed good promise, and the necessary money to cover the dreaded note, due the last of August, was already in the bank. The complicating elements in regard to David were of quite another nature.

To Simeon Holly, the boy was a riddle to be sternly solved. To Ellen Holly, he was an ever-present reminder of the little boy of long ago, and as such was to be loved and trained into a semblance of what that boy might have become. To Perry Larson, David was the "derndest checkerboard of sense and nonsense going"—a game over which to chuckle.

At the Holly farmhouse, they could not understand a boy who would leave a supper for a sunset, or who preferred a book to a toy pistol—as Perry Larson found out was the case on the Fourth of July; who picked flowers, like a girl, for the table; yet who unhesitatingly struck the first blow in a fight with six antagonists, who would not go fishing because the fish would not like it, nor hunting for any sort of wild thing that had life; who hung entranced for an hour over the "millions of lovely striped bugs" in a field of early potatoes; and who promptly and stubbornly refused to sprinkle those same "lovely bugs" with Paris green when discovered at his worship. All this was most perplexing, to say the least.

Yet David worked, and worked well; and, in most cases, he obeyed orders willingly. He learned much, too, that was interesting and profitable, nor was he the only one that made strange discoveries during those July days. The Hollys themselves learned much. They learned that the rose of sunset and the gold of sunrise were worth looking at, and that the massing of the thunderheads in the west meant more than just a shower. They learned, too, that the green of the hilltop and of the far-reaching meadow was more than grass, and that the purple haze along the horizon was more than the mountains that lay between them and the next State. They were beginning to see the world through David's eyes.

There were, too, the long twilights and evenings when David, on the wings of his violin, would speed away to his mountain home, leaving behind him a man and a woman who seemed, to themselves, to be listening to the voice of a curly-headed, rosy-cheeked lad who once played at their knees and nestled in their arms when the day was done. And here, too, the Hollys were learning, though the thing thus learned was hidden deep in their hearts.

It was not long after David's first visit that the boy went again to "The House that Jack Built," as the Gurnseys called their tiny home. (Though in reality it had been Jack's father who had built the house. Jack and Jill, however, did not always deal with realities.) It was not a pleasant afternoon. There was a light mist in the air, and David was without his violin.

"I came to—to inquire for the cat—Juliette," he began, a little bashfully. "I thought I'd rather do that than read today," he explained to Jill in the doorway.

"Good! I'm so glad! I hoped you'd come," the little girl welcomed him. "Come in and—and see Juliette," she added hastily, remembering at the last moment that her brother had not looked with entire favor on her avowed admiration for this strange little boy.

Juliette, roused from her nap, was at first inclined to resent her visitor's presence. In five minutes, however, she was purring in his lap.

The conquest of the kitten once accomplished, David looked about him a little restlessly. He began to wonder why he had come. He wished he had gone to see Joe Glaspell instead. He wished that Jill would not sit and stare at him like that. He wished that she would say something—anything. But Jill, apparently struck dumb with embarrassment, was nervously twisting the corner of her apron into a little knot. David tried to recollect what he had talked about a few days before, and he wondered why he had so enjoyed himself then. He wished that something would happen—anything! And then from an inner room came the sound of a violin.

David raised his head.

"It's Jack," stammered the little girl—who also had been wishing something would happen. "He plays, same as you do, on the violin."

"Does he?" beamed David. "But—" He paused, listening, a quick frown on his face.

Over and over the violin was playing a single phrase, and the variations in the phrase showed the indecision of the fingers and of the mind that controlled them. Again and again, with irritating sameness, yet with a still more irritating difference, came the succession of notes. And then David sprang to his feet, placing Juliette somewhat unceremoniously on the floor, much to that petted young autocrat's disgust.

"Here, where is he? Let me show him," cried the boy, and at the note of command in his voice, Jill involuntarily rose and opened the door to Jack's den.

"Oh, please, Mr. Jack," burst out David, hurrying into the room. "Don't you see? You don't go at that thing right. If you'll just let me show you a minute, we'll have it fixed in no time!"

The man with the violin stared, and then lowered his bow. A slow red came to his face. The phrase was peculiarly a difficult one, and beyond him, as he knew; but that did not make the present intrusion into his privacy any the more welcome.

"Oh, will we, indeed!" he retorted, a little sharply. "Don't trouble yourself, I beg of you, boy."

"But it isn't a mite of trouble, truly," urged David, with an ardor that ignored the sarcasm in the other's words. "I want to do it."

Despite his annoyance, the man gave a short laugh.

"Well, David, I believe you. And I'll warrant you'd tackle this Brahms concerto as nonchalantly as you did those six hoodlums with the cat the other day—and expect to win out, too!"

"But, truly, this is easy, when you know how," laughed the boy. "See!"

To his surprise, the man found himself relinquishing the violin and bow into the slim, eager hands that reached for them. The next moment, he fell back in amazement. Clear, distinct, yet connected like a string of rounded pearls fell the troublesome notes from David's bow.

"You see," smiled the boy again, and played the phrase a second time, more slowly, and with deliberate emphasis at the difficult part. Then, as if in answer to some irresistible summons within him, he dashed into the next phrase and, with marvelous technique, played quite through the rippling cadenza that completed the movement.

"Well, by George!" breathed the man dazedly, as he took the offered violin. The next moment he had demanded vehemently: "Goodness! Who are you, boy?"

David's face wrinkled in grieved surprise.

"Why, I'm David. Don't you remember? I was here just the other day!"

"Yes, yes, but who taught you to play like that?"

"Father."

"'Father'!" The man echoed the word with a gesture of comic despair. "First Latin, then jiujitsu, and now the violin! Boy, who was your father?"

David lifted his head and frowned a little. He had been questioned so often, and so unsympathetically, about his father that he was beginning to resent it.

"He was Daddy—just Daddy, and I loved him dearly."

"But what was his name?"

"I don't know. We didn't seem to have a name like—like yours down here. Anyway, if we did, I didn't know what it was."

"But, David—" The man was speaking very gently now. He had motioned the boy to a low seat by his side. The little girl was standing near, her eyes alight with wondering interest. "He must have had a name, you know, just the same. Didn't you ever hear any one call him anything? Think, now."

"No." David said the single word and turned his eyes away. It had occurred to him, since he had come to live in the valley, that perhaps his father did not want to have his name known. He remembered that once the milk-and-eggs boy had asked what to call him, and his father had laughed and answered: "I don't see but you'll have to call me 'The Old Man of the Mountain,' as they do down in the village." That was the only time David could recollect hearing his father say anything about his name. At the time David had not thought much about it. But since then, down here where they appeared to think a name was so important, he had wondered if possibly his father had not preferred to keep his to himself. If such were the case, he was glad now that he did not know his name, so that he might not have to tell all these inquisitive people who asked so many questions about it. He was glad, too, that those men had not been able to read his father's name at the end of his other note that first morning—if his father really did not wish his name to be known.

"But, David, think. Where you lived, wasn't there ever anybody who called him by name?"

David shook his head. "I told you. We were all alone, Father and I, in the little house far up on the mountain."

"And—your mother?"

Again David shook his head. "She is an angel-mother, and angel-mothers don't live in houses, you know."

There was a moment's pause; then the man asked gently, "And you always lived there?"

"Six years, Father said."

"And before that?"

"I don't remember." There was a touch of injured reserve in the boy's voice which the man was quick to perceive. He took the hint at once.

"He must have been a wonderful man—your father!" he exclaimed.

The boy turned, his eyes luminous with feeling. "He was. He was perfect! But they—down here—don't seem to know—or care," he choked.

"Oh, but that's because they don't understand," soothed the man. "Now, tell me, you must have practiced a lot to play like that."

"I did—but I liked it."

"And what else did you do? And how did you happen to come—down here?"

Once again David told his story, more fully, perhaps, this time than ever before, because of the sympathetic ears that were listening.

"But now," he finished wistfully, "it's all so different, and I'm down here alone. Daddy went, you know, to the far country, and he can't come back from there."

"Who told you that?"

"Daddy himself. He wrote it to me."

"Wrote it to you!" cried the man, sitting suddenly erect.

"Yes. It was in his pocket, you see. They—found it." David's voice was very low, and not quite steady.

"David, may I see that letter?"

The boy hesitated, then slowly drew it from his pocket. "Yes, Mr. Jack. I'll let you see it."

Reverently, tenderly, but very eagerly, the man took the note and read it through, hoping somewhere to find a name that would help solve the mystery. With a sigh, he handed it back. His eyes were wet.

"Thank you, David. That is a beautiful letter," he said softly. "And I believe you'll do it someday, too. You'll go to him with your violin at your chin and the bow drawn across the strings to tell him of the beautiful world you have found."

"Yes, sir," said David simply. Then, with a suddenly radiant smile, "And now I can't help finding it a beautiful world, you know, 'cause I don't count the hours I don't like."

"You don't what? Oh, I remember," returned Mr. Jack, a quick change coming to his face.

"Yes, the sundial, you know, where my Lady of the Roses lives."

"Jack, what is a sundial?" broke in Jill eagerly.

Jack turned, as if in relief. "Hullo, girlie, you there?—and so still all this time? Ask David. He'll tell you what a sundial is. Suppose, anyhow, that you two go out on the piazza now. I've got—er-some work to do. And the sun itself is out, see?—through the trees there. It came out just to say 'goodnight,' I'm sure. Run along, quick!" And he playfully drove them from the room.

Alone, he turned and sat down at his desk. His work was

before him, but he did not do it. His eyes were out of the window on the golden tops of the towers of Sunnycrest. Motionless, he watched them until they turned gray-white in the twilight. Then he picked up his pencil and began to write feverishly. He went to the window, however, as David stepped off the veranda, and called merrily, "Remember, boy, that when there's another note that baffles me, I'm going to send for you."

"He's coming anyhow. I asked him," announced Jill.

And David laughed back a happy "Of course I am!"

CHAPTER 14

The Tower Window

IT IS BE EXPECTED THAT WHEN ONE'S THOUGHTS LEAD SO persistently to a certain place, one's feet will follow, if they can; and David's could—so he went to seek his Lady of the Roses.

At four o'clock one afternoon, with his violin under his arm, he traveled the firm white road until he came to the shadowed path that led to the garden. He had decided that he would go exactly as he went before. He expected, in consequence, to find his Lady exactly as he had found her before, sitting reading under the roses. Great was his surprise and disappointment, therefore, to find the garden with no one in it.

He had told himself that it was the sundial, the roses, the shimmering pool, the garden itself that he wanted to see; but he knew now that it was the lady—his Lady of the Roses. He did not even care to play, though all around him was the beauty that had at first so charmed his eye. Very slowly he walked across the sunlit, empty space and entered the path that led to the house. In his mind was no definite plan; yet he walked on and on until he came to the wide lawns surrounding the house itself. He stopped then, entranced.

Stone upon stone the majestic pile rose until it was etched, clean-cut, against the deep blue of the sky. The towers—his towers—brought to David's lips a cry of delight. They were even more enchanting here than when seen from afar over the treetops, and David gazed up at them in awed wonder. From somewhere came the sound of music—a curious sort of music that David had never heard before. He listened intently, trying to place it; then slowly he crossed the lawn, ascended the imposing stone steps, and softly opened one of the narrow screen doors before the wide-open French window.

Once within the room, David drew a long breath of ecstasy. Beneath his feet he felt the velvet softness of the green moss of the woods. Above his head he saw a sky-like canopy of blue carrying fleecy clouds on which floated little pink-and-white children with wings, just as David himself had so often wished that he could float. On all sides silken hangings, like the green of swaying vines, half-hid other hangings of feathery, snowflake lace. Everywhere mirrored walls caught the light and reflected the potted ferns and palms so that David looked down endless vistas of loveliness that seemed for all the world like the long sun-flecked aisles beneath the tall pines of his mountain home.

The music that David had heard at first had long since stopped, but David had not noticed that. He stood now in the center of the room, awed and trembling, but enraptured. Then from somewhere came a voice—a voice so cold that it sounded as if it had swept across a field of ice.

"Well, boy, when you have quite finished your inspection, perhaps you will tell me to what I am indebted for this visit," it said.

David turned abruptly.

"O Lady of the Roses, why didn't you tell me it was like this—in here?" he breathed.

"Well, really," murmured the lady in the doorway, stiffly, "it had not occurred to me that that was hardly—necessary."

"But it was! Don't you see? This is new, all new. I never saw anything like it before, and I do so love new things. It gives me something new to play. Don't you understand?"

"New to play?"

"Yes, on my violin," explained David a little breathlessly, softly testing his violin. "There's always something new in this, you know," he hurried on, as he tightened one of the strings, "when there's anything new outside. Now, listen! You see, I don't know myself just how it's going to sound, and I'm always so anxious to find out." And with a joyously rapt face, he began to play.

"But, see here, boy, you mustn't! You—" The words died on her lips; and, to her unbounded amazement, Miss Barbara Holbrook, who had intended peremptorily to send this persistent little tramp boy about his business, found herself listening to a melody so compelling in its sonorous beauty that she was left almost speechless at its close. It was the boy who spoke.

"There, I told you my violin would know what to say!"

"'What to say'! Well, that's more than I do," laughed Miss Holbrook, a little hysterically. "Boy, come here and tell me who you are." And she led the way to a low divan that stood near a harp at the far end of the room.

It was the same story, told as David had told it to Jack and Jill a few days before, only this time David's eyes were roving admiringly all about the room, resting oftenest on the harp so near him.

"Did that make the music that I heard?" he asked eagerly, as soon as Miss Holbrook's questions gave him opportunity. "It's got strings."

"Yes. I was playing when you came in. I saw you enter the window. Really, David, are you in the habit of walking into people's houses like this? It is most disconcerting to their owners."

"Yes—no—well, sometimes." David's eyes were still on the harp. "Lady of the Roses, won't you please play again—on that?"

"David, you are incorrigible! Why did you come into my house like this?"

"The music said 'come,' and the towers, too. You see, I know the towers."

"You know them?"

"Yes. I can see them from so many places, and I always watch for them. They show best of anywhere, though, from Jack and Jill's. And now won't you play?"

Miss Holbrook had almost risen to her feet when she turned abruptly. "From—where?" she asked.

"From Jack and Jill's—the House that Jack Built, you know."

"You mean—Mr. John Gurnsey's house?" A deeper color had come into Miss Holbrook's cheeks.

"Yes. Over there at the top of the little hill across the brook, you know. You can't see their house from here, but from over there, we can see the towers finely, and the little window—Oh, Lady of the Roses," he broke off excitedly at the new thought that had come to him, "if we, now, were in that little window, we could see their house. Let's go up. Can't we?"

Explicit as this was, Miss Holbrook evidently did not hear, or at least did not understand, this request. She settled back on the divan, indeed, almost determinedly. Her cheeks were very red now.

"And do you know—this Mr. Jack?" she asked lightly.

"Yes, and Jill, too. Don't you? I like them, too. Do you know them?"

Again Miss Holbrook ignored the question put to her. "And did you walk into their house, unannounced and uninvited, like this?" she queried.

"No, he asked me. You see, he wanted to get off some of the dirt and blood before other folks saw me."

"The dirt and—and—why, David, what do you mean? What was it—an accident?"

David frowned and reflected a moment. "No. I did it on

purpose. I had to, you see," he finally elucidated. "But there were six of them, and I got the worst of it."

"David!" Miss Holbrook's voice was horrified. "You don't mean—a fight!"

"Yes'm. I wanted the cat—and I got it, but I wouldn't have if Mr. Jack hadn't come to help me."

"Oh! So Mr. Jack fought, too?"

"Well, he pulled the others off, and of course that helped me," explained David truthfully. "And then he took me home—he and Jill."

"Jill! Was she in it?"

"No, only her cat. They had tied a bag over its head and a tin can to its tail, and of course I couldn't let them do that. They were hurting her. And now, Lady of the Roses, won't you please play?"

For a moment Miss Holbrook did not speak. She was gazing at David with an odd look in her eyes. At last she drew a long sigh. "David, you are the—the *limit*!" she breathed, as she rose and seated herself at the harp.

David was manifestly delighted with her playing and begged for more when she had finished, but Miss Holbrook shook her head. She seemed to have grown suddenly restless, and she moved about the room calling David's attention to something new each moment. Then, very abruptly, she suggested that they go upstairs. From room to room she hurried the boy, scarcely listening to his ardent comments, or answering his still more ardent questions. Not until they reached the highest tower room, indeed, did she sink wearily into a chair and seem for a moment at rest.

David looked about him in surprise. Even his untrained eye could see that he had entered a different world. There were no sumptuous rugs, no silken hangings, no mirrors, no snowflake curtains. There were books, to be sure, but besides those, there were only a plain low table, a work-basket, and three or four wooden-seated though comfortable chairs. With increasing wonder he looked into Miss Holbrook's eyes.

"Is it here that you stay—all day?" he asked diffidently.

Miss Holbrook's face turned a vivid scarlet. "Why, David, what a question! Of course not! Why should you think I did?"

"Nothing; only I've been wondering all the time I've been here how you could—with all those beautiful things around you down-stairs—say what you did."

"Say what? When?"

"That other day in the garden, about *all* your hours being cloudy ones. So I wondered today if you lived up here—same as Mrs. Holly doesn't use her best rooms—and that was why your hours were all cloudy ones."

With a sudden movement, Miss Holbrook rose to her feet.

"Nonsense, David! You shouldn't always remember everything that people say to you. Come, you haven't seen one of the views from the windows yet. We are in the larger tower, you know. You can see Hinsdale village on this side, and there's a fine view of the mountains over there. Oh yes, and from the other side there's your friend's house—Mr. Jack's. By the way, how is Mr. Jack these days?" Miss Holbrook stooped as she asked the question and picked up a bit of thread from the rug.

David ran at once to the window that looked toward the House that Jack Built. From the tower, the little house appeared to be smaller than ever. It was in the shadow, too, and looked strangely alone and forlorn. Unconsciously, as he gazed at it, David compared it with the magnificence he had just seen. His voice choked as he answered.

"He isn't well, Lady of the Roses, and he's unhappy. He's awfully unhappy."

Miss Holbrook's slender figure came up with a jerk. "What do you mean, boy? How do you know he's unhappy? Has he said so?"

"No, but Mrs. Holly told me about him. He's sick, and he had just found his work to do out in the world when he had to stop and come home. But—oh, quick, there he is! See?"

Instead of coming nearer, Miss Holbrook fell back to the center of the room, but her eyes were still turned toward the little house.

"Yes, I see," she murmured. The next instant, she had snatched a handkerchief from David's outstretched hand. "No, no—I wouldn't wave," she remonstrated hurriedly. "Come—come downstairs with me."

"But I thought—I was sure he was looking this way," asserted David, turning reluctantly from the window. "And if he *had* seen me wave to him, he'd have been so glad; now, wouldn't he?"

There was no answer. The Lady of the Roses did not apparently hear. She had gone on down the stairway.

CHAPTER 15

Secrets

D AVID HAD SO MUCH TO TELL JACK AND JILL THAT HE
went to see them the very next day after his second visit
to Sunnycrest. He carried his violin with him. He found,
however, only Jill at home. She was sitting on the veranda steps.

There was not so much embarrassment between them this
time, perhaps because they were in the freedom of the wide
outdoors, and David felt more at ease. He was plainly disap-
pointed, however, that Mr. Jack was not there.

"But I wanted to see him! I wanted to see him 'specially," he
lamented.

"You'd better stay then. He'll be home by and by," comforted Jill.
"He's gone pot-boiling."

"Pot-boiling! What's that?"

Jill chuckled.

"Well, you see, really it's this way: he sells something to boil in
other people's pots so he can have something to boil in ours, he
says. It's stuff from the garden, you know. We raise it to sell. Poor
Jack—and he does hate it so!"

David nodded sympathetically. "I know—and it must be awful,
just hoeing and weeding all the time."

"Still, of course, he knows he's got to do it, because it's outdoors,
and he just has to be outdoors all he can," rejoined the girl. "He's
sick, you know, and sometimes he's so unhappy! He doesn't say

much. Jack never says much—only with his face. But I know, and it—it just makes me want to cry."

At David's dismayed exclamation, Jill jumped to her feet. She suddenly realized that she was telling this unknown boy altogether too many of the family secrets. She proposed at once a race to the foot of the hill; and then, to drive David's mind still farther away from the subject under recent consideration, she deliberately lost and proclaimed him the victor.

Very soon, however, there arose new complications in the shape of a little gate that led to a path which, in its turn, led to a footbridge across the narrow span of the little stream. Above the trees on the other side peeped the top of Sunnycrest's highest tower.

"To the Lady of the Roses!" cried David eagerly. "I know it goes there. Come, let's see!"

The little girl shook her head. "I can't."

"Why not?"

"Jack won't let me."

"But it goes to a beautiful place. I was there yesterday," argued David. "And I was up in the tower and almost waved to Mr. Jack on the piazza back there. I saw him. And maybe she'd let you and me go up there again today."

"But I can't, I say," repeated Jill, a little impatiently. "Jack won't let me even start."

"Why not? Maybe he doesn't know where it goes to."

Jill hung her head. Then she raised it defiantly. "Oh, yes, he does, 'cause I told him. I used to go when I was littler and he wasn't here. I went once after he came—halfway—and he saw me and called to me. I had got halfway across the bridge, but I had to come back. He was very angry, yet sort of—strange, too. His face was all stern and white, and his lips snapped tight shut after every word. He said never, never, never to let him find me the other side of that gate."

David frowned as they turned to go up the hill. Unhesitatingly, he determined to instruct Mr. Jack in this little matter. He would tell him what a beautiful place Sunnycrest was, and he would try to convince him how very desirable it was that he and Jill, and even Mr. Jack himself, should go across the bridge at the very first opportunity.

Mr. Jack came home before long, but David quite forgot to speak of the footbridge just then, chiefly because Mr. Jack got out his violin and asked David to come in and play a duet with him. The duet, however, soon became a solo, for so great was Mr. Jack's delight in David's playing that he placed before the boy one sheet of music after another, begging and still begging for more.

David, nothing loath, played on and on. Most of the music he knew, having already learned it in his mountain home. Like old friends the melodies seemed, and so glad was David to see their notes again that he finished each production with a little improvised cadenza of ecstatic welcome—to Mr. Jack's increasing surprise and delight.

"Great Scott! You're a wonder, David," he exclaimed, at last.

"Pooh! as if that was anything wonderful," laughed the boy. "Why, I knew those ages ago, Mr. Jack. It's only that I'm so glad to see them again—the notes, you know. You see, I haven't any music now. It was all in the bag that we brought and left on the way."

"You left it?"

"Yes, it was so, heavy," murmured David distractedly, his fingers busy with the pile of music before him. "Oh, and here's another one," he cried exultingly. "This is where the wind sighs, 'oou—OOU—OOU' through the pines. Listen!" And he was away again on the wings of his violin. When he had returned, Mr. Jack drew a long breath.

"David, you are a wonder," he declared again. "And that violin of yours is a wonder, too, if I'm not mistaken—though I don't know enough to tell whether it's really a rare one or not. Was it your father's?"

"Oh, no. He had one, too, and they both are good ones. Father said so. Joe's got Father's violin now."

"Joe?"

"Joe Glaspell."

"You don't mean Widow Glaspell's Joe, the blind boy? I didn't know he could play."

"He couldn't till I showed him. But he likes to hear me play. And he understood—right away, I mean."

"Understood?"

"What I was playing, you know. And he was almost the first one that did since Father went away. And now I play every time I go there. Joe says he never knew before how trees and grass and sunsets and sunrises and birds and little brooks did look, till I told him with my violin. Now he says he thinks he can see them better than I can, because as long as his outside eyes can't see anything, they can't see those ugly things all around him, and so he can just make his inside eyes see only the beautiful things that he'd like to see. And that's the kind he does see when I play. That's why I said he understood."

For a moment there was silence. In Mr. Jack's eyes there was an odd look as they rested on David's face. Then, abruptly, he spoke. "David, I wish I had money. Then I'd put you where you belonged," he sighed.

"Do you mean—where I'd find my work to do?" asked the boy softly.

"Well, yes, you might say it that way," smiled the man, after a moment's hesitation. Mr. Jack was not yet quite used to this boy who was at times so very un-boylike.

"Father told me it was waiting for me—somewhere."

Mr. Jack frowned thoughtfully.

"And he was right, David. The only trouble is, we like to pick it out for ourselves, pretty well—too well, as we find out sometimes, when we're called off—for another job."

"I know, Mr. Jack, I know," breathed David. And the man, looking into the glowing dark eyes, wondered at what he found there. It was almost as if the boy really understood about his own life's disappointment—and cared, though that, of course, could not be!

"And it's all the harder to keep ourselves in tune then, too, isn't it?" went on David, a little wistfully.

"In tune?"

"With the rest of the Orchestra."

"Oh!" And Mr. Jack, who had already heard about the "Orchestra of Life," smiled a bit sadly. "That's just it, my boy. And if we're handed another instrument to play on rather than the one we want to play on, we're apt to—to let fly a discord. Anyhow, I am." He went on more lightly, "But now, in your case, David, little as I know about the violin, I know enough to understand that you ought to be where you can take up your study of it again, where you can hear good music, and where you can be among those who know enough to appreciate what you do."

David's eyes sparkled. "And where there wouldn't be any pulling weeds or hoeing dirt?"

"Well, I hadn't thought of including either of those pastimes."

"My, but I would like that, Mr. Jack! But that wouldn't be work, so that couldn't be what Father meant." David's face fell.

"Hmm. Well, I wouldn't worry about the 'work' part," laughed Mr. Jack, "particularly as you aren't going to do it just now. There's the money, you know—and we haven't got that."

"And it takes money?"

"Well, yes. You can't get those things here in Hinsdale, you know; and it takes money to get away, and to live away after you get there."

A sudden light transfigured David's face. "Mr. Jack, would gold do it? Lots of little round gold pieces?"

"I think it would, David, if there were enough of them."

"As many as a hundred?"

"Sure, if they were big enough. Anyway, David, they'd start you, and I'm thinking you wouldn't need but a start before you'd be coining gold pieces of your own out of that violin of yours. But why? Anybody you know got as 'many as a hundred' gold pieces he wants to get rid of?"

For a moment David, his delighted thoughts flying to the gold pieces in the chimney cupboard of his room, was tempted to tell his secret. Then he remembered the woman with the bread and the pail of milk and decided not to. He would wait. When he knew Mr. Jack better—perhaps then he would tell, but not now. Now Mr. Jack might think he was a thief, and that he could not bear. So he took up his violin and began to play; and in the charm of the music, Mr. Jack seemed to forget the gold pieces, which was exactly what David had intended should happen.

Not until David had said goodbye some time later, did he remember the purpose—the special purpose—for which he had come. He turned back with a radiant face.

"Oh, and Mr. Jack, I almost forgot," he cried. "I was going to tell you. I saw you yesterday—I did, and I almost waved to you."

"Did you? Where were you?"

"Over there in the window—the tower window," he crowed jubilantly.

"Oh, you went again then, I suppose, to see Miss Holbrook."

The man's voice sounded so oddly cold and distant that David noticed it at once. He was reminded suddenly of the gate and the footbridge which Jill was forbidden to cross, but he dared not speak of it then—not when Mr. Jack looked like that. He did say, however, "Oh, but, Mr. Jack, it's such a beautiful place! You don't know what a beautiful place it is."

"Is it? Then, you like it so much?"

"Oh, so much! But—didn't you ever—see it?"

"Why, yes, I believe I did, David, long ago," murmured Mr. Jack with what seemed to David amazing indifference.

"And did you see HER—my Lady of the Roses?"

"Why, yes, I believe so."

"And is that all you remember about it?" resented David, highly offended.

The man gave a laugh, a little short, hard laugh that David did not like. "But, let me see; you said you almost waved, didn't you? Why didn't you, quite?" asked the man.

David drew himself suddenly erect. Instinctively, he felt that his Lady of the Roses needed defense. "Because she didn't want me to; so I didn't, of course," he rejoined with dignity. "She took away my handkerchief."

"I'll warrant she did," muttered the man, behind his teeth. Aloud, he only laughed again as he turned away.

David went on down the steps, dissatisfied vaguely with himself, with Mr. Jack, and even with the Lady of the Roses.

CHAPTER 16

David's Castle in Spain

O N HIS RETURN FROM THE HOUSE THAT JACK BUILT, DAVID decided to count his gold pieces. He got them out at once from behind the books and stacked them up in little shining rows. As he had surmised, there were a hundred of them. There were, indeed, a hundred and six. He was pleased at that. One hundred and six were surely enough to give him a "start."

A start! David closed his eyes and pictured it. To go on with his violin, to hear good music, to be with people who understood what he said when he played! That was what Mr. Jack had said a "start" was. And this gold—these round, shining bits of gold— could bring him this! David swept the little piles into a jingling heap and sprang to his feet with both fists full of his suddenly beloved wealth. With boyish glee, he capered about the room, jingling the coins in his hands. Then, very soberly, he sat down again and began to gather the gold to put away.

He would be wise. He would be sensible. He would watch his chance, and when it came, he would go away. First, however, he would tell Mr. Jack, and Joe, and the Lady of the Roses; yes, and the Hollys, too. Just now there seemed to be work, real work that he could do to help Mr. Holly. But later, possibly when September came and school—they had said he must go to school—he would tell them and go away instead. He would see. By that time they would believe him, perhaps, when he showed the gold pieces. They would not think he had stolen them. It was August now; he would wait. But meanwhile, he could think—he could always be thinking of the wonderful thing that this gold was one day to bring to him.

Even work, to David, did not seem work now. In the morning he was to rake hay behind the men with the cart. Yesterday he had not liked it very well; but now—nothing mattered now. And with a satisfied sigh, David put his precious gold away again behind the books in the cupboard.

David found a new song in his violin the next morning. To be sure, he could not play it—much of it—until four o'clock in the afternoon came; for Mr. Holly did not like violins to be played in the morning, even on days that were not especially the Lord's. There was too much work to do. So David could only snatch a strain or two very, very softly, while he was dressing; but that was enough to show him what a beautiful song it was going to be. He knew at once what it was, too. It was the gold pieces and what they would bring. All through the day, it tripped through his consciousness and danced tantalizingly just out of reach. Yet he was wonderfully happy, and the day seemed short in spite of the heat and the weariness.

At four o'clock, he hurried home and put his violin quickly in tune. It came then—that dancing sprite of tantalization—and joyously abandoned itself to the strings of the violin, so that David knew, of a surety, what a beautiful song it was.

It was this song that sent him the next afternoon to see his Lady of the Roses. This time he found her outdoors in her garden. Unceremoniously, as usual, he rushed headlong into her presence.

"Oh, Lady—Lady of the Roses," he panted. "I've found out, and I came quickly to tell you."

"Why, David, what—what do you mean?" Miss Holbrook looked unmistakably startled.

"About the hours, you know—the unclouded ones," explained

David eagerly. "You know you said they were ALL cloudy to you."

Miss Holbrook's face grew very white. "You mean you've found out why my hours are—are all cloudy ones?" she stammered.

"No, oh, no. I can't imagine why they are," returned David, with an emphatic shake of his head. "It's just that I've found a way to make all my hours sunny ones, and you can do it, too. So I came to tell you. You know you said yours were all cloudy."

"Oh," ejaculated Miss Holbrook, falling back into her old listless attitude. Then, with some asperity, she added, "Dear me, David! Didn't I tell you not to be remembering that all the time?"

"Yes, I know, but I've *learned* something," urged the boy, "something that you ought to know. You see, I did think, once, that because you had all these beautiful things around you, the hours ought to be all sunny ones. But now I know it isn't what's around you, it's what is *in* you!"

"Oh, David, David, you curious boy!"

"No, but really! Let me tell you," pleaded David. "You know I haven't liked them—all those hours till four o'clock came— and I was so glad, after I saw the sundial, to find out that they didn't count, anyhow. But today they HAVE counted—they've all counted, Lady of the Roses; and it's just because there was something inside of me that shone and shone, and made them all sunny—those hours."

"Dear me! And what was this wonderful thing?"

David smiled, but he shook his head. "I can't tell you that yet— in words, but I'll play it. You see, I can't always play them twice alike—those little songs that I find—but this one I can. It sang so long in my head, before my violin had a chance to tell me what it really was, that I sort of learned it. Now, listen!" And he began to play.

It was, indeed, a beautiful song, and Miss Holbrook said so with promptness and enthusiasm; yet still David frowned.

"Yes, yes," he answered, "but don't you see? That was telling you about something inside of me that made all my hours sunshiny ones. Now, what you want is something inside of you to make yours sunshiny, too. Don't you see?"

An odd look came into Miss Holbrook's eyes.

"That's all very well for you to say, David, but you haven't told me yet, you know, just what it is that's made all this brightness for you."

The boy changed his position and puckered his forehead into a deeper frown. "I don't seem to explain so you can understand," he sighed. "It isn't the special thing. It's only that it's something. And it's thinking about it that does it. Now, mine wouldn't make yours shine, but still—" he broke off, a happy relief in his eyes, "yours could be like mine, in one way. Mine is something that is going to happen to me, something just beautiful. And you could have that, you know—something that was going to happen to you, to think about."

Miss Holbrook smiled but only with her lips. Her eyes had grown somber.

"But there isn't anything 'just beautiful' that is going to happen to me, David," she demurred.

"There could be, couldn't there?"

Miss Holbrook bit her lip; then she gave an odd little laugh that seemed, in some way, to go with the swift red that had come to her cheeks.

"I used to think there could be—once," she admitted. "But I've given that up long ago. It—it didn't happen."

"But couldn't you just think it was going to?" persisted the boy. "You see, I found out yesterday that it's the thinking that does it. All day long I was thinking—only thinking. I wasn't doing it at all. I was really raking behind the cart, but the hours all were sunny."

Miss Holbrook laughed now outright.

"What a persistent little mental-science preacher you are!" she exclaimed. "And there's truth—more truth than you know—in it all, too. But I can't do it, David. Not that—not that. It would take more than thinking to bring that," she added under her breath, as if to herself.

"But thinking does bring things," maintained David earnestly. "There's Joe—Joe Glaspell. His mother works out all day, and he's blind."

"Blind? Oh!" shuddered Miss Holbrook.

"Yes, and he has to stay all alone, except for Betty, and she isn't there much. He thinks all his things. He has to. He can't see anything with his outside eyes, but he sees everything with his inside eyes—everything that I play. Why, Lady of the Roses, he's even seen this—all this here. I told him about it, you know, right away after I'd found you that first day: the big trees, and the long shadows across the grass, and the roses, and the shining water, and the lovely marble people peeping through the green leaves, and the sundial, and you—so beautiful—sitting here in the middle of it all. Then I played it for him, and he said he could see it all just as plain! And that was with his inside eyes! And so, if Joe, shut up there in his dark little room, can make his Think bring him all that, I should think that you, here in this beautiful, beautiful place, could make your Think bring you anything you wanted it to."

But Miss Holbrook sighed again and shook her head.

"Not that, David, not that," she murmured. "It would take more than thinking to bring—that." Then, with a quick change of manner, she cried: "Come, come! Suppose we don't worry any more about my hours. Let's think of yours. Tell me, what have you been doing since I saw you last? Perhaps you have been again to—to see Mr. Jack, for instance."

"I have, but I saw Jill mostly, till the last." David hesitated, then he blurted it out: "Lady of the Roses, do you know about the gate and the footbridge?"

Miss Holbrook looked up quickly.

"Know—what, David?"

"Know about them—that they're there?"

"Why, yes, of course. At least, I suppose you mean the footbridge that crosses the little stream at the foot of the hill over there."

"That's the one." Again David hesitated, and again he blurted out the burden of his thoughts. "Lady of the Roses, did you ever cross that bridge?"

Miss Holbrook stirred uneasily.

"Not recently."

"But you don't mind folks crossing it?"

"Certainly not—if they wish to."

"There! I knew it wasn't your blame," triumphed David.

"MY blame!"

"Yes, that Mr. Jack wouldn't let Jill come across, you know. He called her back when she'd got halfway over once." Miss Holbrook's face changed color.

"But I do object," she cried sharply, "to their crossing it when they don't want to! Don't forget that, please."

"But Jill did want to."

"How about her brother? Did he want her to?"

"N—no."

"Very well, then. I didn't, either."

David frowned. Never had he seen his beloved Lady of the Roses look like this before. He was reminded of what Jill had said about Jack: "His face was all stern and white, and his lips snapped tight shut after every word." So, too, looked Miss Holbrook's face. So, too, had her lips snapped tightly shut after her last words. David could not understand it. He said nothing more, however;

but, as was usually the case when he was perplexed, he picked up his violin and began to play. And as he played, there gradually came to Miss Holbrook's eyes a softer light, and to her lips lines less tightly drawn. Neither the footbridge nor Mr. Jack, however, was mentioned again that afternoon.

CHAPTER 17

"The Princess & the Pauper"

I T WAS IN THE EARLY TWILIGHT THAT MR. JACK TOLD THE
story. He, Jill, and David were on the veranda, as usual
watching the towers of Sunnycrest turn from gold to silver as
the sun dropped behind the hills. It was Jill who had asked for the
story.

"About princesses, you know," she had ordered.

"But how will David like that?" Mr. Jack had demurred. "Maybe
he doesn't care for princesses."

"I read a story once about a prince—It was *The Prince and the
Pauper*, and I liked that," averred David stoutly.

Mr. Jack smiled, and then his brows drew together in a frown.
His eyes were moodily fixed on the towers.

"Hmm," he said. "Well, I might, I suppose, tell you a story about
a Princess and a Pauper. I know one well enough."

"Good! Then tell it," cried both Jill and David. And Mr. Jack
began his story.

"She was not always a princess, and he was not always a
pauper—and that's where the story came in, I suppose," sighed
the man. "She was just a girl, once, and he was a boy; and they
played together and—liked each other. He lived in a little house
on a hill."

"Like this?" demanded Jill.

"Eh? Oh—er—yes, something like this," returned Mr. Jack, with an odd half-smile. "And she lived in another bit of a house in a town far away from the boy."

"Then how could they play together?" questioned David.

"They couldn't, not always. It was only summers when she came to visit in the boy's town. She was very near him then, for the old aunt whom she visited lived in a big stone house with towers, on another hill, in plain sight from the boy's home."

"Towers like those—where the Lady of the Roses lives?" asked David.

"Eh? What? Oh—er—yes," murmured Mr. Jack. "We'll say the towers were something like those over there." He paused, then went on musingly: "The girl used to signal, sometimes, from one of the tower windows. One wave of the handkerchief meant, 'I'm coming over'; two waves, with a little pause between, meant, 'You are to come over here.' So the boy used to wait always, after that first wave to see if another followed, so that he might know whether he was to be host or guest that day. The waves always came at eight o'clock in the morning, and very eagerly the boy used to watch for them all through the summer when the girl was there."

"Did they always come, every morning?" asked Jill.

"No, sometimes the girl had other things to do. Her aunt would want her to go somewhere with her, or other cousins were expected whom the girl must entertain; and she knew the boy did not like other guests to be there when he was, so she never asked him to come over at such times. On such occasions she did sometimes run up to the tower at eight o'clock and wave three times, and that meant, 'Dead Day.' So the boy, after all, never drew a real breath of relief until he made sure that no dreaded third wave was to follow the one or the two."

"Seems to me," observed David, "that all this was sort of one-sided. Didn't the boy say anything?"

"Oh, yes," smiled Mr. Jack. "But the boy did not have any tower to wave from, you must remember. He had only the little piazza on his tiny bit of a house. But he rigged up a pole, and he asked his mother to make him two little flags, a red and a blue one. The red meant 'All right'; and the blue meant 'Got to work'; and these he used to run up on his pole in answer to her waving 'I'm coming over', or 'You are to come over here'. So, you see, occasionally, it was the boy who had to bring the 'Dead Day' as there were times when he had to work. And, by the way, perhaps you would be interested to know that, after a while, he thought up a third flag to answer her three waves. He found an old black silk handkerchief of his father's, and he made that into a flag. He told the girl it meant 'I'm heartbroken', and he said it was a sign of the deepest mourning. The girl laughed and tipped her head saucily to one side, and said, 'Pooh! As if you really cared!' But the boy stoutly maintained his position, and it was that, perhaps, which made her play the little joke one day.

"The boy was fourteen that summer, and the girl thirteen. They had begun their signals years before, but they had not had the black one so long. On this day that I tell you of, the girl waved three waves, which meant, 'Dead Day', you remember, and watched until the boy had hoisted his black flag which said, 'I'm heartbroken', in response. Then, as fast as her mischievous little feet could carry her, she raced down one hill and across to the other. Very stealthily she advanced till she found the boy bent over a puzzle on the back stoop, and—and he was whistling merrily.

"How she teased him then! How she taunted him with 'Heartbroken, indeed—and whistling like that!' In vain he blushed and stammered and protested that his whistling was only to keep up his spirits. The girl only laughed and tossed her yellow curls; then she hunted till she found some little jingling bells, and these she tied to the black badge of mourning and pulled it high up on the flagpole. The next instant, she was off with a run and a skip, and a saucy wave of her hand; and the boy was left all alone with an hour's work ahead of him to untie the knots from his desecrated badge of mourning.

"And yet they were wonderfully good friends—this boy and girl. From the very first, when they were seven and eight, they had said that they would marry each other when they grew up, and always they spoke of it as the expected thing, and laid many happy plans for the time when it should come. To be sure, as they grew older, it was not mentioned quite so often, perhaps; but the boy at least thought—if he thought of it all—that that was only because it was already so well understood."

"What did the girl think?" It was Jill who asked the question.

"Eh? The girl? Oh," answered Mr. Jack, a little bitterly, "I'm afraid I don't know exactly what the girl did think, but—it wasn't that, anyhow—that is, judging from what followed."

"What did follow?"

"Well, to begin with, the old aunt died. The girl was sixteen then. It was in the winter that this happened, and the girl was far away at school. She came to the funeral, however, but the boy did not see her, save in the distance; and then he hardly knew her, so strange did she look in her black dress and hat. She was there only two days, and though he gazed wistfully up at the gray tower, he knew well enough that, of course, she could not wave to him at such a time as that. Yet he had hoped—almost believed—that she would wave two waves that last day, and let him go over to see her.

"But she didn't wave, and he didn't go over. She went away. And then the town learned a wonderful thing. The old lady, her aunt, who had been considered just fairly rich, turned out to be the possessor of almost fabulous wealth, owing to her great holdings of stock in a Western gold mine which had suddenly struck it rich. And to the girl she willed it all. It was then, of course, that the girl became the Princess, but the boy did not realize that—just then. To him, she was still 'the girl.'

"For three years he did not see her. She was at school or traveling abroad, he heard. He, too, had been away to school, and was, indeed, just ready to enter college. Then, that summer, he heard that she was coming to the old home, and his heart sang within him. Remember, to him she was still the girl. He knew, of course, that she was not the little girl who had promised to marry him. But he was sure she was the merry comrade, the true-hearted young girl who used to smile frankly into his eyes, and whom he was now to win for his wife. You see he had forgotten—quite forgotten—about the Princess and the money. Such a foolish, foolish boy as he was!

"So he got out his flags gleefully, and one day, when his mother wasn't in the kitchen, he ironed out the wrinkles and smoothed them all ready to be raised on the pole. He would be ready when the girl waved—for, of course, she would wave; he would show her that he had not forgotten. He could see just how the sparkle would come to her eyes, and just how the little fine lines of mischief would crinkle around her nose when she was ready to give that first wave. He could imagine that she would like to find him napping, that she would like to take him by surprise and make him scurry around for his flags to answer her.

"But he would show her! As if she, a girl, were to beat him at their old game! He wondered which it would be: 'I'm coming over,' or, 'You are to come over here.' Whichever it was, he would answer, of course, with the red 'All right.' Still, it would be a joke to run up the blue 'Got to work,' and then slip across to see her, just as she, so long ago, had played the joke on him! On the whole, however, he thought the red flag would be better. And it was that one which he laid uppermost ready to his hand, when he arranged them.

"At last she came. He heard of it at once. It was already past four o'clock, but he could not forbear, even then, to look toward the tower. It would be like her, after all, to wave then, that very night, just so as to catch him napping, he thought. She did not wave, however. The boy was sure of that, for he watched the tower till dark.

"In the morning, long before eight o'clock, the boy was ready. He debated for some time whether to stand out of doors on the piazza or to hide behind the screened window where he could still watch the tower. He decided, at last, that it would be better not to let her see him when she looked toward the house; then his triumph would be all the more complete when he dashed out to run up his answer.

"Eight o'clock came and passed. The boy waited until nine, but there was no sign of life from the tower. The boy was angry then, at himself. He called himself, indeed, a fool, to hide as he did. Of course, she wouldn't wave when he was nowhere in sight—when he had apparently forgotten! And here was a whole precious day wasted!

"The next morning, long before eight, the boy stood in plain sight on the piazza. As before, he waited until nine, and as before, there was no sign of life at the tower window. The next morning he was there again, and the next, and the next. It took just five days, indeed, to convince the boy—as he was convinced at last—that the girl did not intend to wave at all."

"But how unkind of her!" exclaimed David.

"She couldn't have been nice one bit!" decided Jill.

"You forget," said Mr. Jack. "She was the Princess."

"Huh!" grunted Jill and David in unison.

"The boy remembered it then," went on Mr. Jack, after a pause, "—about the money, and that she was a Princess. And of course he knew, when he thought of it, that he could not expect that a Princess would wave like a girl—just a girl. Besides, very likely she did not care particularly about seeing him. Princesses did forget, he fancied—they had so much, so very much to fill their lives. It was this thought that kept him from going to see her—this, and the recollection that, after all, if she really HAD wanted to see him, she could have waved.

"There came a day, however, when another youth, who did not dare to go alone, persuaded him, and together they paid her a call. The boy understood, then, many things. He found the Princess; there was no sign of the girl. The Princess was tall and dignified, with a cold little hand and a smooth, sweet voice. There was no frank smile in her eyes, neither were there any mischievous crinkles about her nose and lips. There was no mention of towers or flags, no reference to waving or to childhood's days. There was only a stiffly polite little conversation about colleges and travels, with a word or two about books and plays. Then the callers went home. On the way, the boy smiled scornfully to himself. He was trying to picture the beauteous vision he had seen, this unapproachable Princess in her filmy lace gown—standing in the tower window and waving—waving to a bit of a house on the opposite hill. As if that could happen!

"The boy, during those last three years, had known only books. He knew little of girls—only one girl—and he knew still less of Princesses. So when, three days after the call, there came a chance to join a summer camp with a man who loved books even better than did the boy himself, he went gladly. Once he had refused to go on this very trip, but then there had been the girl. Now there was only the Princess—and the Princess didn't count."

"Like the hours that aren't sunshiny," interpreted David.

"Yes," corroborated Mr. Jack. "Like the hours when the sun doesn't shine."

"And then?" prompted Jill.

"Well, then—there wasn't much worth telling," rejoined Mr.

Jack gloomily. "Two more years passed, and the Princess grew to be twenty-one. She came into full control of her property then, and after a while, she came back to the old stone house with the towers and turned it into a land of beauty. She spent money like water. All manner of artists, from the man who painted her ceilings to the man who planted her seeds, came and bowed to her will. From the four corners of the earth, she brought her treasures and lavished them through the house and grounds. Then, every summer, she came herself and lived among them, a very Princess indeed."

"And the boy? What became of the boy?" demanded David. "Didn't he see her—ever?"

Mr. Jack shook his head. "Not often, David. And when he did, it did not make him any happier. You see, the boy had become the Pauper; you mustn't forget that."

"But he wasn't a Pauper when you left him last."

"Wasn't he? Well, then, I'll tell you about that. You see, the boy, even though he did go away, soon found out that in his heart the Princess was still the girl, just the same. He loved her, and he wanted her to be his wife; so for a little—for a very little—he was wild enough to think that he might work and study and do great things in the world until he was even a Prince himself, and then he could marry the Princess."

"Well, couldn't he?"

"No. To begin with, he lost his health. Then, away back in the little house on the hill something happened—a something that left a very precious charge for him to keep; and he had to go back and keep it, and to try to see if he couldn't find that lost health, as well. And that is all."

"All! You don't mean that that is the end!" exclaimed Jill.

"That's the end."

"But that isn't a mite of a nice end," complained David. "They always get married and live happy ever after—in stories."

"Do they?" Mr. Jack smiled a little sadly. "Perhaps they do, David—in stories."

"Well, can't they in this one?"

"I don't see how."

"Why can't he go to her and ask her to marry him?"

Mr. Jack drew himself up proudly. "The Pauper and the Princess? Never! Paupers don't go to Princesses, David, and say, 'I love you.'"

David frowned. "Why not? I don't see why—if they want to do it. Seems as if somehow it might be fixed."

"It can't be," returned Mr. Jack, his gaze on the towers that crowned the opposite hill; "not so long as always before the Pauper's eyes there are those gray walls behind which he pictures the Princess in the midst of her golden luxury."

To neither David nor Jill did the change to the present tense seem strange. The story was much too real to them for that.

"Well, anyhow, I think it ought to be fixed," declared David, as he rose to his feet.

"So do I—but we can't fix it," laughed Jill. "And I'm hungry. Let's see what there is to eat!"

CHAPTER 18

David to the Rescue

I T WAS A BEAUTIFUL MOONLIT NIGHT, BUT FOR ONCE DAVID was not thinking of the moon. All the way to the Holly farmhouse he was thinking of Mr. Jack's story, "The Princess and the Pauper." It held him strangely. He felt that he never could forget it. For some reason that he could not have explained, it made him sad, too, and his step was very quiet as he went up the walk toward the kitchen door.

It was after eight o'clock. David had taken supper with Mr. Jack and Jill, and not for some hours had he been at the farmhouse. In the doorway now he stopped short; then, instinctively, he stepped back into the shadow. In the kitchen a kerosene light was burning. It showed Mrs. Holly crying at the table, and Mr. Holly, white-faced and stern-lipped, staring at nothing. Then Mrs. Holly raised her face, drawn and tear-stained, and asked a trembling question.

"Simeon, have you thought? We might go—to John—for—help."

David was frightened then, so angry was the look that came into Simeon Holly's face.

"Ellen, we'll have no more of this," said the man harshly. "Understand, I'd rather lose the whole thing and—and starve, than go to—John."

David fled then. Up the back stairs he crept to his room and left his violin. A moment later he stole down again and sought Perry

Larson, whom he had seen smoking in the barn doorway.

"Perry, what is it?" he asked in a trembling voice. "What has happened—in there?" He pointed toward the house.

The man puffed for a moment in silence before he took his pipe from his mouth. "Well, sonny, I s'pose I may as well tell you. You'll have to know it sometime, seein' as it won't be no secret long. They've had some bad news—Mr. and Miss Holly has."

"What is it?"

"Well, it's money—and one might as well talk moonshine to you as money, I s'pose; but here goes it. It's a thousand dollars, boy, that they owed. Here, like this," he explained, rummaging his pockets until he had found a silver dollar to lay on his open palm. "Now, jest imagine a thousand of them; that's heaps and heaps— more 'n I ever see in my life."

"Like the stars?" guessed David.

The man nodded.

"Ex-*actly*! Well, they owed this—Mr. and Mis' Holly did—and they had agreed to pay it next Saturday. And they was all right, too. They had it plum saved in the bank, and was going' to draw it Thursday, to make sure, and they was feelin' mighty pert over it, too, when today along comes the news that something's broke kersmash in that bank, and they've shut it up. And not a cent can the Hollys git now—an' maybe never. Anyhow, not 'fore it's too late for this job."

"But won't he wait?—that man they owe it to? I should think he'd have to, if they didn't have it to pay."

"Not much he will, when it's old Streeter that's got the mortgage on a good fat farm like this!"

David drew his brows together perplexedly. "What is a—a mortgage?" he asked. "Is it anything like a *porte-cochere*? I know what that is, 'cause my Lady of the Roses has one; but we haven't got that—down here."

Perry Larson sighed in exasperation. "That's about what I expected of ye! No, it ain't even second cousin to a—a-that thing you're a-talkin' of. In plain wordin', it's jest this: Mr. Holly, he says to Streeter: 'You give me a thousand dollars, and I'll pay ye back on a sartin day; if I don't pay, you can sell my farm fur what it'll bring, and *take* yer pay. Well, now here it is. Mr. Holly can't pay, and so Streeter will put up the farm fur sale."

"What, with Mr. and Mrs. Holly living here?"

"Sure! Only they'll have to git out, ye know."

"Where'll they go?"

"The Lord knows; I don't."

"And is that what they're crying for—in there? Because they've got to go?"

"Sure!"

"But isn't there anything, anywhere, that can be done to stop it?"

"I don't see how, kid—not unless someone ponies up with the money 'fore next Saturday—an' a thousand o' them things don't grow on ev'ry bush," he finished, gently patting the coin in his hand.

At the words, a swift change came to David's face. His cheeks paled and his eyes dilated in terror. It was as if ahead of him he saw a yawning abyss, eager to engulf him.

"And you say—*money* would—fix it?" he asked thickly.

"Ex-*act*-ly!—a thousand o' them, though, it would take."

A dawning relief came into David's eyes—it was as if he saw a bridge across the abyss.

"You mean—that there wouldn't anything do, only silver pieces—like those?" he questioned hopefully.

"Sugar, kid, 'course there would! You be a checkerboard o' sense and nonsense, and no mistake! Any money would do the job—any money! Don't ye see? Anything that's money."

"Would g-gold do it?" David's voice was very faint now.

"Sure! Gold or silver or greenbacks, or—or a check, if it had the dough behind it."

David did not appear to hear the last. With an oddly strained look, he had hung upon the man's first words, but at the end of the sentence he only murmured, "Oh, thank you," and turned away. He was walking slowly now toward the house. His head was bowed. His step lagged.

"Now, ain't that jest like that chap," muttered the man, "to slink off like that as if he was a whipped cur. I'll bet two cents and a doughnut, too, that in five minutes he'll be what he calls 'playing it' on that 'ere fiddle o' his, and I'll be derned, too, if I ain't curious to see what he will make of it. It strikes me this ought to fetch something first cousin to a dirge!"

David paused on the porch steps for a breathless instant. From the kitchen came the sound of Mrs. Holly's sobs and of a stern voice praying. With a shudder and a little choking cry, the boy turned then and crept softly upstairs to his room.

He played, too, as Perry Larson had wagered. But it was not the tragedy of the closed bank, nor the horror of the threatened farm-selling that fell from his violin. It was, instead, the swan song of a little pile of gold—gold which lay now in a chimney cupboard, but which was soon to be placed at the feet of the mourning man and woman downstairs. And in the song was the sob of a boy who sees his house of dreams burn to ashes, who sees his wonderful life and work out in the wide world turn to endless days of weed-pulling and dirt-digging in a narrow valley. There was in the song, too, something of the struggle, the fierce yea and nay of the conflict. But, at the end, there was the wild burst of exaltation of renunciation, so that the man in the barn door below fairly sprang to his feet with an angry "He's turned the thing into a jig! Don't he know more'n that at such a time as this?"

Later, a very little later, the shadowy figure of the boy stood before him.

"I've been thinking," stammered David, "that maybe I—could help, about that money, you know."

"Now, look a-here, boy," exploded Perry, in open exasperation, "as I said in the first place, this ain't in your class. It ain't no pink cloud sailin' in the sky, nor a bluebird singing' in a blackb'rry bush, and you might 'play it'—as you call it—till doomsday, and it wouldn't do no good—though I'm free to confess that your playing of them 'ere other things sounds real pert and chirky at times; but it won't do no good here."

David stepped forward, bringing his small, anxious face full into the moonlight.

"But it was the money, Perry; I meant about the money," he explained. "They were good to me and wanted me when there wasn't anyone else that did; and now I'd like to do something for them. There aren't so many pieces, and they aren't silver. There's only one hundred and six of them; I counted. But maybe they'd help some. It—it would be a—start." His voice broke over the once beloved word, then went on with renewed strength. "There, see! Would these do?" And with both hands, he held up to view his cap sagging under its weight of gold.

Perry Larson's jaw fell open. His eyes bulged. Dazedly he reached out and touched with trembling fingers the heap of shining disks that seemed in the mellow light like little earth-born children of the moon itself. The next instant he recoiled sharply.

"Great snakes, boy, where'd you git that money?" he demanded.

"From my father. He went to the far country, you know."

Perry Larson snorted angrily.

"See here, boy, for once, if ye can, talk horse-sense! Surely, even you don't expect me to believe that he's sent you that money from—from where he's gone to!"

"Oh, no. He left it."

"Left it! Why, boy, you know better! There wasn't a cent, hardly, found on him."

"He gave it to me before—by the roadside."

"Gave it to you! Where in the name of goodness has it been since?"

"In the little cupboard in my room, behind the books."

"Great snakes!" muttered Perry Larson, reaching out his hand and gingerly picking up one of the gold pieces.

David eyed him anxiously.

"Won't they—do?" he faltered. "There aren't a thousand; there's only a hundred and six, but—"

"Do!" cut in the man, excitedly. He had been examining the gold piece at close range. "Do! Well, I reckon they'll do. By Jiminy! And to think you've had this up yer sleeve all this time! Well, I'll believe anythin' of yer now—anythin'! You can't stump me with nuthin'! Come on." And he hurriedly led the way toward the house.

"But they weren't up my sleeve," corrected David, as he tried to keep up with the long strides of the man. "I said they were in the cupboard in my room."

There was no answer. Larson had reached the porch steps and had paused there, hesitating. The sound of sobs still came from the kitchen. Aside from that there was silence. The boy, however, did not hesitate. He went straight up the steps and through the open kitchen door. At the table sat the man and the woman, their eyes covered with their hands.

With a swift overturning of his cap, David dumped his burden onto the table and stepped back respectfully. "If you please, sir, would this help any?" he asked.

At the jingle of the coins, Simeon Holly and his wife lifted their heads abruptly. A half-uttered sob died on the woman's lips. A quick cry came from the man's. He reached forth an eager hand and had almost clutched the gold when a sudden change came to his face. With a stern word he drew back.

"Boy, where did that money come from?" he challenged.

David sighed in a discouraged way. It seemed that, always, the showing of this gold meant questioning—eternal questioning.

"Surely," continued Simeon Holly, "you did not—" With the boy's frank gaze upturned to his, the man could not finish his sentence.

Before David could answer came the voice of Perry Larson from the kitchen doorway. "No, sir, he didn't, Mr. Holly, and it's all straight, I'm thinkin'—though I'm free to confess it does sound nutty. His dad give it to him."

"His—father! But where—where has it been ever since?"

"In the chimney cupboard in his room, he says, sir."

Simeon Holly turned in frowning amazement. "David, what does this mean? Why have you kept this gold in a place like that?"

"Why, there wasn't anything else to do with it," answered the boy perplexedly. "I hadn't any use for it, you know, and Father said to keep it till I needed it."

"'Hadn't any use for it'!" blustered Larson from the doorway. "Jiminy! Now, ain't that jest like that boy?"

But David hurried on with his explanation. "We never used to use them—Father and I—except to buy things to eat and wear; and down here you give me those, you know."

"Do you reckon, boy, that Mr. Holly himself was given them things he gives to you?" interjected Perry Larson.

The boy turned sharply, a startled question in his eyes. "What do you mean? Do you mean that—" His face changed suddenly. His cheeks turned a shamed red. "Why, he did—he did have to buy them, of course, just as Father did. And I never even thought of it before! Then, it's yours, anyway—it belongs to you," he argued, turning to Farmer Holly and shoving the gold nearer to his hands. "There isn't enough, maybe, but it will help!"

"They're ten-dollar gold pieces, sir," spoke up Larson importantly, "an' there's a hundred and six of them. That's jest one thousand and sixty dollars, as I make it."

Simeon Holly, self-controlled man that he was, almost leaped from his chair.

"One thousand and sixty dollars!" he gasped. Then, to David: "Boy! Who are you?"

"I don't know—only David." The boy spoke wearily, with a grieved sob in his voice. He was very tired, a good deal perplexed, and a little angry. He wished, if no one wanted this gold, that he could take it upstairs again to the chimney cupboard; or, if they objected to that, that they would at least give it to him and let him go away now to that beautiful music he was to hear, and to those kind people who were always to understand what he said when he played.

"Of course," ventured Perry Larson diffidently, "I ain't professin' to know any great shakes about the hand of the Lord, Mr. Holly, but it do strike me that this 'ere gold comes mighty near bein' providential—fur you."

Simeon Holly fell back in his seat. His eyes clung to the gold, but his lips set into rigid lines.

"That money is the boy's, Larson. It isn't mine," he said.

"He's given it to you."

Simeon Holly shook his head. "David is nothing but a child, Perry. He doesn't realize at all what he is doing, nor how valuable his gift is."

"I know, sir, but you did take him in when there wouldn't nobody else do it," argued Larson. "An', anyhow, couldn't you make a kind of an IOU of it, even if he is a kid? Then someday you could pay him back. Meanwhile, you'd be a-keepin' him, and a-schoolin' him."

"I know, I know," nodded Simeon Holly thoughtfully, his eyes going from the gold to David's face. Then, aloud, yet as if to himself, he breathed: "Boy, boy, who was your father? How came he by all that gold—and he—a tramp!"

David drew himself suddenly erect. His eyes flashed. "I don't know, sir. But I do know this: he didn't steal it!"

Across the table Mrs. Holly drew a quick breath, but she did not speak—save with her pleading eyes. Mrs. Holly seldom spoke save with her eyes when her husband was solving a knotty problem. She was dumbfounded now that he should listen so patiently to the man, Larson, though she was not more surprised than was Larson himself. For both of them, however, there came at this moment a still greater surprise. Simeon Holly leaned forward suddenly, the stern lines quite gone from his lips and his face working with emotion as he drew David toward him.

"You're a good son, boy—a good loyal son; and—and I wish you were mine! I believe you. He didn't steal it, and I won't steal it, either. But I will use it, since you are so good as to offer it. But it shall be a loan, David, and some day, God helping me, you shall have it back. Meanwhile, you're my boy, David—my boy!"

"Oh, thank you, sir," rejoiced David. "And, really, you know, being wanted like that is better than the start would be, isn't it?"

"Better than—what?"

David shifted his position. He had not meant to say just that. "N—nothing," he stammered, looking about for a means of quick escape. "I—I was just talking," he finished. And he was immeasurably relieved to find that Mr. Holly did not press the matter further.

CHAPTER 19

The Unbeautiful World

IN SPITE OF THE EXALTATION OF RENUNCIATION, AND IN SPITE of the joy of being newly and especially "wanted," those early September days were sometimes hard for David. Not until he had relinquished all hope of his "start" did he fully realize what that hope had meant to him.

There were times, to be sure, when there was nothing but rejoicing within him that he was able thus to aid the Hollys. There were other times when there was nothing but the sore heartache because of the great work out in the beautiful world that could now never be done, and because of the unlovely work at hand that must be done. To tell the truth, indeed, David's entire conception of life had become suddenly a chaos of puzzling contradictions.

To Mr. Jack, one day, David went with his perplexities. Not that he told him of the gold pieces and of the unexpected use to which they had been put—indeed, no. David had made up his mind never, if he could help himself, to mention those gold pieces to any one who did not already know of them. They meant questions, and the questions, explanations. And he had had enough of both on that particular subject. But to Mr. Jack he said one day, when they were alone together, "Mr. Jack, how many folks have you got inside of your head?"

"Eh—what, David?"

David repeated his question and attached an explanation. "I

mean, the folks that—that make you do things."

Mr. Jack laughed. "Well," he said, "I believe some people make claims to quite a number, and perhaps almost everyone owns to a Dr. Jekyll and a Mr. Hyde."

"Who are they?"

"Never mind, David. I don't think you know the gentlemen, anyhow. They're only something like the little girl with a curl. One is very, very good, indeed, and the other is horrid."

"Oh, yes, I know them; they're the ones that come to me," returned David, with a sigh. "I've had them a lot, lately."

Mr. Jack stared. "Oh, have you?"

"Yes, and that's what's the trouble. How can you drive them off—the one that is bad, I mean?"

"Well, really," confessed Mr. Jack, "I'm not sure I can tell. You see—the gentlemen visit me sometimes."

"Oh, do they?"

"Yes."

"I'm so glad—that is, I mean," amended David, in answer to Mr. Jack's uplifted eyebrows, "I'm glad that you understand what I'm talking about. You see, I tried Perry Larson last night on it, to get him to tell me what to do, but he only stared and laughed. He didn't know the names of 'em, anyhow, as you do, and at last he got really almost angry and said I made him feel so 'buggy' and 'creepy' that he wouldn't dare look at himself in the glass if I kept on, for fear someone he'd never known was there should jump out at him."

Mr. Jack chuckled. "Well, I suspect, David, that Perry knew one of your gentlemen by the name of 'Conscience,' perhaps; and I also suspect that maybe Conscience does pretty nearly fill the bill, and that you've been having a bout with that. Eh? Now, what is the trouble? Tell me about it."

David stirred uneasily. Instead of answering, he asked another question. "Mr. Jack, it is a beautiful world, isn't it?"

For a moment there was no, answer; then a low voice replied, "Your father said it was, David."

Again David moved restlessly. "Yes, but Father was on the mountain. And down here—well, down here there are lots of things that I don't believe he knew about."

"What, for instance?"

"Why, lots of things—too many to tell. Of course there are things like catching fish, and killing birds and squirrels and other things to eat, and plaguing cats and dogs. Father never would have called those beautiful. Then there are others like little Jimmy Clark who can't walk, and the man at the Marstons' who's sick, and Joe Glaspell who is blind. Then there are still different ones like Mr. Holly's little boy. Perry says he ran away years and years ago, and made his people very unhappy. Father wouldn't call that a beautiful world, would he? And how can people like that always play in tune? And there are the Princess and the Pauper that you told about."

"Oh, the story?"

"Yes, and people like them can't be happy and think the world is beautiful, of course."

"Why not?"

"Because they didn't end right. They didn't get married and live happy ever after, you know."

"Well, I don't think I'd worry about that, David—at least, not about the Princess. I fancy the world was very beautiful to her, all right. The Pauper—well, perhaps he wasn't very happy. But, after all, David, you know happiness is something inside of yourself. Perhaps half of these people are happy, in their way."

"There! And that's another thing," sighed David. "You see, I found that out—that it was inside of yourself—quite a while ago, and I told the Lady of the Roses. But now I—I can't make it work myself."

"What's the matter?"

"Well, you see then something was going to happen—something that I liked, and I found that just thinking of it made it so that I didn't mind raking or hoeing, or anything like that; and I told the Lady of the Roses. And I told her that, even if it wasn't going to happen, she could *think* it was going to, and that that would be just the same, because it was the thinking that made my hours sunny ones. It wasn't the doing at all. I said I knew because I hadn't done it yet. See?"

"I think so, David."

"Well, I've found out that it isn't the same at all; for now that I know that this beautiful thing isn't ever going to happen to me, I can think and think all day, and it doesn't do a mite of good. The sun is just as hot, and my back aches just as hard, and the field is just as big and endless as it used to be when I had to call it that those hours didn't count. Now, what is the matter?"

Mr. Jack laughed, but he shook his head a little sadly.

"You're getting into too deep waters for me, David. I suspect you're floundering in a sea that has upset the boats of sages since the world began. But what is it that was so nice, and that isn't going to happen? Perhaps I might help on that."

"No, you couldn't," frowned David. "And there couldn't anybody, either, you see, because I wouldn't go back now and let it happen, anyhow, as long as I know what I do. Why, if I did, there wouldn't be any hours that were sunny then, not even the ones after four o'clock. I—I'd feel so mean! But what I don't see is just how I can fix it up with the Lady of the Roses."

"What has she to do with it?"

"Why, at the very first, when she said she didn't have any sunshiny hours, I told her—"

"When she said what?" interposed Mr. Jack, coming suddenly erect in his chair.

"That she didn't have any hours to count, you know."

"To—count?"

"Yes, it was the sundial. Didn't I tell you? Yes, I know I did—about the words on it—not counting any hours that weren't sunny, you know. And she said she wouldn't have any hours to count, that the sun never shone for her."

"Why, David," demurred Mr. Jack in a voice that shook a little, "are you sure? Did she say just that? You—you must be mistaken—when she has—has everything to make her happy."

"I wasn't, because I said that same thing to her myself afterwards. And then I told her—when I found out myself, you know—about its being what was inside of you, after all, that counted; and then is when I asked her if she couldn't think of something nice that was going to happen to her sometime."

"Well, what did she say?"

"She shook her head, and said 'No.' Then she looked away, and her eyes got soft and dark like little pools in the brook where the water stops to rest. And she said she had hoped once that this something would happen; but that it hadn't, and that it would take something more than thinking to bring it. And I know now what she meant, because thinking isn't all that counts, is it?"

Mr. Jack did not answer. He had risen to his feet and was pacing restlessly up and down the veranda. Once or twice he turned his eyes toward the towers of Sunnycrest, and David noticed that there was a new look on his face.

Very soon, however, the old tiredness came back to his eyes, and he dropped into his seat again, muttering, "Fool! Of course it couldn't be—that!"

"Be what?" asked David.

Mr. Jack started. "Er—nothing; nothing that you would understand, David. Go on with what you were saying."

"There isn't any more. It's all done. It's only that I'm wondering how I'm going to learn here that it's a beautiful world, so that I can tell Father."

Mr. Jack roused himself. He had the air of a man who determinedly throws to one side a heavy burden. "Well, David," he smiled, "as I said before, you are still out on that sea where there are so many little upturned boats. There might be a good many ways of answering that question."

"Mr. Holly says," mused the boy aloud, a little gloomily, "that it doesn't make any difference whether we find things beautiful or not; that we're here to do something serious in the world."

"That is about what I should have expected of Mr. Holly," retorted Mr. Jack grimly. "He acts it—and looks it. But I don't believe you are going to tell your father just that."

"No, sir, I don't believe I am," accorded David soberly.

"I have an idea that you're going to find that answer just where your father said you would—in your violin. See if you don't. Things that aren't beautiful, you'll make beautiful—because we find what we are looking for, and you're looking for beautiful things. After all, boy, if we march straight ahead, chin up, and sing our own little song with all our might and main, we shan't come so far amiss from the goal, I'm thinking. There! That's preaching, and I didn't mean to preach, but—well, to tell the truth, that was meant for myself, for—I'm hunting for the beautiful world, too."

"Yes, sir, I know," returned David fervently. And again Mr. Jack, looking into the sympathetic, glowing dark eyes, wondered if, after all, David really could—know.

Even yet Mr. Jack was not used to David; there were "so many of him," he told himself. There were the boy, the artist, and a third personality so evanescent that it defied being named. The boy was jolly, impetuous, confidential, and delightful—plainly reveling in all manner of fun and frolic. The artist was nothing but a bunch of nervous alertness, ready to find melody and rhythm in every passing thought or flying cloud. The third—that baffling third that defied the naming—was a dreamy, visionary, untouchable creature who floated so far above one's head that one's hand could never pull him down to get a good square chance to see what he did look like. Mr. Jack thought all of this as he gazed into David's luminous eyes.

CHAPTER 20

The Unfamiliar Way

IN SEPTEMBER DAVID ENTERED THE VILLAGE SCHOOL. School and David did not assimilate at once. Very confidently, the teacher set to work to grade her new pupil, but she was not so confident when she found that while in Latin he was perilously near herself (and in French—which she was not required to teach—disastrously beyond her!). In United States history, he knew only the barest outlines of certain portions and could not name a single battle in any of its wars. In most studies he was far beyond boys of his own age, yet at every turn, she encountered these puzzling spots of discrepancy, which rendered grading in the ordinary way out of the question.

David's methods of recitation, too, were peculiar, and somewhat disconcerting. He also did not hesitate to speak aloud when he chose, nor to rise from his seat and move to any part of the room as the whim seized him. In time, of course, all this was changed, but it was several days before the boy learned so to conduct himself that he did not shatter to atoms the peace and propriety of the schoolroom.

Outside of school David had little work to do now, though there were still left a few light tasks about the house. Home life at the Holly farmhouse was the same for David, yet with a difference—the difference that comes from being really wanted instead of being merely dutifully kept. There were other differences, too, subtle differences that did not show, perhaps, but that still were there.

Mr. and Mrs. Holly, more than ever now, were learning to look at the world through David's eyes. One day—one wonderful day— they even went to walk in the woods with the boy, and whenever before had Simeon Holly left his work for so frivolous a thing as a walk in the woods?

It was not accomplished, however, without a struggle, as David could have told. The day was a Saturday, clear, crisp, and beautiful, with a promise of October in the air; and David fairly tingled to be free and away. Mrs. Holly was baking—and the birds sang unheard outside her pantry window. Mr. Holly was digging potatoes—and the clouds sailed unnoticed above his head.

All the morning David urged and begged. If for once, just this once, they would leave everything and come, they would not regret it, he was sure. But they shook their heads and said, "No, no, impossible!" In the afternoon the pies were done and the potatoes dug, and David urged and pleaded again. If once, only this once, they would go to walk with him in the woods, he would be so happy, so very happy! And to please the boy—they went.

It was a curious walk. Ellen Holly trod softly, with timid feet. She threw hurried, frightened glances from side to side. It was plain that Ellen Holly did not know how to play. Simeon Holly stalked at her elbow, stern, silent, and preoccupied. It was plain that Simeon Holly not only did not know how to play but did not even care to find out.

The boy tripped ahead and talked. He had the air of a monarch displaying his kingdom. On one side was a bit of moss worthy of the closest attention, and on another, a vine that carried allure-ment in every tendril. Here was a flower that was like a story for interest, and there was a bush that bore a secret worth the telling. Even Simeon Holly glowed into a semblance of life when

David had unerringly picked out and called by name the spruce, and fir, and pine, and larch, and then, in answer to Mrs. Holly's murmured: "But, David, where's the difference? They look so much alike!" he had said, "Oh, but they aren't, you know. Just see how much more pointed at the top that fir is than that spruce back there; and the branches grow straight out, too, like arms, and they're all smooth and tapering at the ends like a pussycat's tail. But the spruce back there—its branches turned down and out—didn't you notice?—and they're all bushy at the ends like a squirrel's tail. Oh, they're lots different! That's a larch way ahead—that one with the branches all scraggly and close down to the ground. I could start to climb that easy, but I couldn't that pine over there. See, it's way, way up before there's a place for your foot! But I love pines. Up there on the mountains where I lived, the pines were so tall that it seemed as if God used them sometimes to hold up the sky."

And Simeon Holly heard and said nothing, and that he did say nothing—especially nothing in answer to David's confident assertions concerning celestial and terrestrial architecture—only goes to show how well, indeed, the man was learning to look at the world through David's eyes.

Nor were these all of David's friends to whom Mr. and Mrs. Holly were introduced on that memorable walk. There were the birds and the squirrels, and, in fact, everything that had life. And each one he greeted joyously by name, as he would greet a friend whose home and habits he knew. Here was a wonderful wood-pecker, there was a beautiful blue jay. Ahead, that brilliant bit of color that flashed across their path was a tanager. Once, far up in the sky as they crossed an open space, David spied a long black streak moving southward.

"Oh, see!" he exclaimed. "The crows! See them?—way up there? Wouldn't it be fun if we could do that, and fly hundreds and hundreds of miles, maybe a thousand?"

"Oh, David," remonstrated Mrs. Holly, unbelievingly.

"But they do! These look as if they'd started on their winter journey south, too; but if they have, they're early. Most of them don't go till October. They come back in March, you know. Though I've had them, on the mountain, that stayed all the year with me."

"My, but I love to watch them go," murmured David, his eyes following the rapidly disappearing black line. "Lots of birds you can't see, you know, when they start for the South. They fly at night—the woodpeckers and orioles and cuckoos, and lots of others. They're afraid, I guess, don't you? But I've seen them. I've watched them. They tell each other when they're going to start."

"Oh, David," remonstrated Mrs. Holly, again, her eyes reproving but plainly enthralled.

"But they do tell each other," claimed the boy, with sparkling eyes. "They must! For, all of a sudden, some night, you'll hear the signal, and then they'll begin to gather from all directions. I've seen them. Then suddenly they're all up and off to the south—not in one big flock, but broken up into little flocks, following one after another, with such a beautiful whir of wings. Oof—OOF—OOF!—and they're gone! And I don't see them again till next year. But you've seen the swallows, haven't you? They go in the daytime, and they're the easiest to tell of any of them. They fly so swift and straight. Haven't you seen the swallows go?"

"Why, I—I don't know, David," murmured Mrs. Holly, with a helpless glance at her husband stalking on ahead. "I—I didn't know there were such things to—to know."

There was more, much more, that David said before the walk came to an end. And though, when it did end, neither Simeon Holly nor his wife said a word of its having been a pleasure or a profit, there was yet on their faces something of the peace and rest and quietness that belonged to the woods they had left.

It was a beautiful month—that September, and David made the

most of it. Out of school meant out of doors for him. He saw Mr. Jack and Jill often. He spent much time, too, with the Lady of the Roses. She was still the Lady of the Roses to David, though in the garden now were the purple and scarlet and yellow of the asters, salvia, and golden glow, instead of the blush and perfume of the roses.

David was very much at home at Sunnycrest. He was welcome, he knew, to go where he pleased. Even the servants were kind to him, as well as was the elderly cousin whom he seldom saw, but who, he knew, lived there as company for his Lady of the Roses.

Perhaps best, next to the garden, David loved the tower room, possibly because Miss Holbrook herself so often suggested that they go there. And it was there when he said, dreamily, one day, "I like this place—up here so high—only sometimes it does make me think of that Princess, because it was in a tower like this that she was, you know."

"Princess stories, David?" asked Miss Holbrook lightly.

"No, not exactly, though there was a Princess in it. Mr. Jack told it." David's eyes were still out of the window.

"Oh, Mr. Jack! And does Mr. Jack often tell you stories?"

"No. He never told only this one—and maybe that's why I remember it so."

"Well, and what did the Princess do?" Miss Holbrook's voice was still light, still carelessly preoccupied. Her attention, plainly, was given to the sewing in her hand.

"She didn't do, and that's what was the trouble," sighed David. "She didn't wave, you know."

The needle in Miss Holbrook's fingers stopped short in mid-air, the thread half-drawn.

"Didn't—wave?" she stammered. "What do you—mean?"

"Nothing," laughed the boy, turning away from the window. "I forgot that you didn't know the story."

"But maybe I do—that is—what was the story?" asked Miss Holbrook, wetting her lips as if they had grown suddenly very dry.

"Oh, do you? I wonder now! It wasn't 'The *Prince* and the Pauper,' but The *Princess* and the Pauper," cited David, "and they used to wave signals and answer with flags. *Do* you know the story?"

There was no answer. Miss Holbrook was putting away her work, hurriedly, and with hands that shook. David noticed that she even pricked herself in her anxiety to get the needle tucked away. Then she drew him to a low stool at her side.

"David, I want you to tell me that story, please," she said, "just as Mr. Jack told it to you. Now, be careful and put it all in, because I—I want to hear it," she finished, with an odd little laugh that seemed to bring two bright red spots to her cheeks.

"Oh, do you want to hear it? Then I will tell it," cried David joyfully. To David, almost as delightful as to hear a story was to tell one himself. "You see, first—" And he plunged headlong into the introduction.

David knew it well, that story; and there was, perhaps, little that he forgot. It might not have been always told in Mr. Jack's language, but his meaning was there, and very intently Miss Holbrook listened while David told of the boy and the girl, the waving, and the flags that were blue, black, and red. She laughed once—that was at the little joke with the bells that the girl played—but she did not speak until sometime later when David was telling of the first home-coming of the Princess, and of the time when the boy on his tiny piazza watched and watched in vain for a waving white signal from the tower.

"Do you mean to say," interposed Miss Holbrook then, almost starting to her feet, "that that boy expected—" She stopped suddenly, and fell back in her chair. The two red spots on her cheeks had become a rosy glow now, all over her face.

"Expected what?" asked David.

"N—nothing. Go on. I was so—so interested," explained Miss Holbrook faintly. "Go on."

And David did go on, nor did the story lose by his telling. It gained something, indeed, for now it had woven through it the very strong sympathy of a boy who loved the Pauper for his sorrow and hated the Princess for causing that sorrow.

"And so," he concluded mournfully, "you see it isn't a very nice story, after all, for it didn't end well a bit. They ought to have got married and lived happy ever after. But they didn't."

Miss Holbrook drew in her breath a little uncertainly and put her hand to her throat. Her face now, instead of being red, was very white.

"But, David," she faltered, after a moment, "perhaps he—the—Pauper—did not—not love the Princess any longer."

"Mr. Jack said that he did."

The white face went suddenly pink again. "Then, why didn't he go to her and—and—tell her?"

David lifted his chin. With all his dignity he answered, and his words and accent were Mr. Jack's. "Paupers don't go to Princesses and say 'I love you.'"

"But perhaps if they did—that is—if—" Miss Holbrook bit her lips and did not finish her sentence. She did not, indeed, say anything more for a long time. But she had not forgotten the story. David knew that, because later she began to question him carefully about many little points—points that he was very sure he had already made quite plain. She talked about it, indeed, until he wondered if perhaps she was going to tell it to someone else sometime. He asked her if she was, but she only shook her head. And after that, she did not question him any more. And a little later David went home.

CHAPTER 21

Heavy Hearts

FOR A WEEK DAVID HAD NOT BEEN NEAR THE HOUSE THAT Jack Built, and that, too, when Jill had been confined within doors for several days with a cold. Jill, indeed, was inclined to be grieved at this apparent lack of interest on the part of her favorite playfellow; but upon her return from her first day of school, after her recovery, she met her brother with startled eyes.

"Jack, it hasn't been David's fault at all," she cried remorsefully. "He's sick."

"Sick!"

"Yes, awfully sick. They've had to send away for doctors and everything."

"Why, Jill, are you sure? Where did you hear this?"

"At school today. Everyone was talking about it."

"But what is the matter?"

"Fever—some sort. Some say it's typhoid, and some scarlet, and some say another kind that I can't remember; but everybody says he's awfully sick. He got it down to Glaspell's, some say—and some say he didn't. But, anyhow, Betty Glaspell has been sick with something, and they haven't let folks in there this week," finished Jill, her eyes big with terror.

"The Glaspells? But what was David doing down there?"

"Why, you know—he told us once—teaching Joe to play. He's been there lots. Joe is blind, you know, and can't see, but he just loves music and was crazy over David's violin; so David took down his other one—the one that was his father's, you know—and showed him how to pick out little tunes, just to take up his time so he wouldn't mind so much that he couldn't see. Now, Jack, wasn't that just like David? Jack, I can't have anything happen to David!"

"No, dear, no, of course not! I'm afraid we can't any of us, for that matter," sighed Jack, his forehead drawn into anxious lines. "I'll go down to the Hollys' the first thing tomorrow morning, and see how he is and if there's anything we can do. Meanwhile, don't take it too much to heart, dear. It may not be half so bad as you think. School children always get things like that exaggerated, you must remember," he finished, speaking with a lightness that he did not feel.

To himself, the man owned that he was troubled, seriously troubled. He had to admit that Jill's story bore the earmarks of truth; and overwhelmingly he realized now just how big a place this somewhat puzzling small boy had come to fill in his own heart. He did not need Jill's anxious, "Now, hurry, Jack," the next morning to start him off in all haste for the Holly farmhouse. A dozen rods from the driveway, he met Perry Larson and stopped him abruptly.

"Good morning, Larson. I hope this isn't true—what I hear—that David is very ill."

Larson pulled off his hat and with his free hand sought the one particular spot on his head to which he always appealed when he was very much troubled.

"Well, yes, sir, I'm afraid it is, Mr. Jack—er—Mr. Gurnsey, I mean. He is terrible sick, poor little chap, and it's too bad—that's what it is—too bad!"

"Oh, I'm sorry! I hoped the report was exaggerated. I came down to see if—if there wasn't something I could do."

"Well, 'course you can ask. There ain't no law again' that; and ye needn't be afraid, neither. The report has got 'round that it's ketchin'—what he's got, and that he got it down to the Glaspells'; but it ain't so. The doctor says he didn't ketch nothing, and he can't give nothing. It's his head and brain that ain't right, and he's got a mighty bad fever. He's been kind of flighty and nervous anyhow, lately.

"As I was saying, 'course you can ask, but I'm thinkin' there won't be nothing you can do to help. Ev'rythin' that can be done is bein' done. In fact, there ain't much of anythin' else that is bein' done down there jest now but tendin' to him. They've got one o' them 'ere edyercated nurses from the Junction—what wears caps, ye know, and makes yer feel as if they knew it all, and you didn't know nothing. And then there's Mr. and Mis' Holly besides. If they had *their* way, there wouldn't neither of em let him out o' their sight fur a minute, they're that cut up about it."

"I fancy they think a good deal of the boy—as we all do," murmured the younger man, a little unsteadily.

Larson wrinkled his forehead in deep thought. "Yes, and that's what beats me," he answered slowly. "About *him*—Mr. Holly, I mean. 'course we'd a-expected it of her—losing her own boy as she did, and being jest naturally so sweet and loving-hearted. But *him*—that's diff'rent. Now, you know jest as well as I do what Mr. Holly is—everyone does, so I ain't saying nothing sland'rous. He's a good man—a powerful good man, and there ain't a squarer man going to work fur. But the fact is, he was made up wrong-side out, and the seams has always showed bad—terrible bad, with ravelin's all stickin' out every which way to ketch and pull. But I'm blamed if that 'ere boy ain't got him so smoothed down you wouldn't know that he had a seam on him sometimes. Though how he's done it beats me. Now, there's Mis' Holly—she's tried to smooth 'em, I'll warrant, lots of times. But I'm free to say she hain't never so much as clipped a ravelin' in all them forty years they've lived together.

Fact is, it's worked the other way with her. All that her rubbin' up against them seams has amounted to is to git herself so smoothed down that she don't never dare to say her soul's her own, most generally—anyhow, not if he happens to intermate it belongs to anybody else!"

Jack Gurnsey suddenly choked over a cough. "I wish I could— do something," he murmured uncertainly.

"It isn't likely ye can—not so long as Mr. and Mis' Holly is on their two feet. Why, there ain't nothing they won't do, and you'll believe it, maybe, when I tell you that yesterday Mr. Holly, he tramped all through Sawyer's woods in the rain jest to find a little bit of moss that the boy was calling for. Think o' that, will ye? Simeon Holly hunting moss! And he got it, too, and brought it home, and they say it cut him up something terrible when the boy just turned away and didn't take no notice. You understand, 'course, sir, the little chap ain't right in his head, and so half the time he don't know what he says."

"Oh, I'm so sorry!" exclaimed Gurnsey, as he turned away, and hurried toward the farmhouse.

Mrs. Holly herself answered his low knock. She looked worn and pale.

"Thank you, sir," she said gratefully, in reply to his offer of assistance, "but there isn't anything you can do, Mr. Gurnsey. We're having everything done that can be, and everyone is very kind. We have a very good nurse, and Dr. Kennedy has had consultation with Dr. Benson from the Junction. They are doing all in their power, of course, but they say that—that it's going to be the nursing that will count now."

"Then I don't fear for him, surely," declared the man, with fervor.

"I know, but—well, he shall have the very best possible—of that."

"I know he will, but isn't there anything—anything that I can do?"

She shook her head.

"No. Of course, if he gets better—" She hesitated, then lifted her chin a little higher. "*When* he gets better," she corrected with courageous emphasis, "he will want to see you."

"And he shall see me," asserted Gurnsey. "And he will be better, Mrs. Holly—I'm sure he will."

"Yes, yes, of course, only—oh, Mr. Jack, he's so sick—so very sick! The doctor says he's a peculiarly sensitive nature, and that he thinks something's been troubling him lately." Her voice broke.

"Poor little chap!" Mr. Jack's voice, too, was husky.

She looked up with swift gratefulness for his sympathy. "And you loved him, too, I know," she choked. "He talks of you often—very often."

"Indeed I love him! Who could help it?"

"There couldn't anybody, Mr. Jack—and that's just it. Now, since he's been sick, we've wondered more than ever who he is. You see, I can't help thinking that somewhere he's got friends who ought to know about him—now."

"Yes, I see," nodded the man.

"He isn't an ordinary boy, Mr. Jack. He's been trained in lots of ways—about his manners, and at the table, and all that. And lots of things his father has told him are beautiful, just beautiful! He isn't a tramp. He never was one. And there's his playing. You know how he can play."

"Indeed, I do! You must miss his playing, too."

"I do. He talks of that, also," she hurried on, working her fingers nervously together. "But oftenest he—he speaks of singing, and I can't quite understand that, for he didn't ever sing, you know."

"Singing? What does he say?" The man asked the question because he saw that it was affording the overwrought little woman real relief to free her mind; but at the first words of her reply, he became suddenly alert.

"It's 'his song,' as he calls it, that he always talks about. It isn't much—what he says—but I noticed it because he always says the same thing, like this: 'I'll just hold up my chin and march straight on and on, and I'll sing it with all my might and main.' And when I ask him what he's going to sing, he always says, 'My song—my song,' just like that. Do you think, Mr. Jack, he did have—a song?"

For a moment the man did not answer. Something in his throat tightened and held the words. Then, in a low voice he managed to stammer, "I think he did, Mrs. Holly, and—I think he sang it, too." The next moment, with a quick lifting of his hat and a murmured, "I'll call again soon," he turned and walked swiftly down the driveway.

So very swiftly, indeed, was Mr. Jack walking, and so self-absorbed was he, that he did not see the carriage until it was almost upon him; then he stepped aside to let it pass. What he saw as he gravely raised his hat was a handsome span of black horses, a liveried coachman, and a pair of startled eyes looking straight into his. What he did not see was the quick gesture with which Miss Holbrook almost ordered her carriage stopped the minute it had passed him by.

CHAPTER 22

As Perry Saw It

ONE BY ONE THE DAYS PASSED, AND THERE CAME FROM the anxious watchers at David's bedside only the words, "There's very little change." Often Jack Gurnsey went to the farmhouse to inquire after the boy. Often, too, he saw Perry Larson; and Perry was never loath to talk of David. It was from Perry, indeed, that Gurnsey began to learn some things of David that he had never known before.

"It does beat all," Perry Larson said to him one day, "how many folks asks me how that boy is—folks that you'd never think knew him, anyhow, to say nothing of carin' whether he lived or died. Now, there's old Mis' Somers, for instance. *You* know what she is— sour as a lemon and puckery as a chokecherry. Well, if she didn't give me yesterday a great boquet o' posies she'd grown herself, and said they was for him—that they belonged to him, anyhow.

" Of course, I didn't exactly sense what she meant by that, so I asked her straight out; and it seems that somehow, when the boy first came, he struck her place one day and spied a great big red rose on one of her bushes. It seems he had his fiddle, and he played it—that rose a-growin' (you know his way!), and she heard and spoke up pretty sharp and asked him what in time he was doing. Well, most kids would-a run—knowing her temper as they does—but not much David. He stands up, as pert as ye please, and tells her how happy that red rose must be to make all that dreary garden look so pretty; and then he goes on, merry as a lark, a-playing down the hill.

"Well, Mis' Somers owned up to me that she was pretty mad at the time, 'cause her garden did look like tunket, and she knew it. She said she hadn't cared to do a thing with it since her Bessie died that thought so much of it. But after what David had said, even mad as she was, the thing kind o' got on her nerves, and she couldn't see a thing, day or night, but that red rose a-growin' there so pert and courageous-like, until at last, jest to quiet herself, she fairly had to set to and slick that garden up! She said she raked and weeded, and fixed up all the plants there was, in good shape, and then she sent down to the Junction for some all grew in pots, 'cause it was too late to plant seeds. And, now it's doing beautiful, so she jest couldn't help sending them posies to David. When I told Mis' Holly, she said she was glad it happened, because what Mis' Somers needed was something to git her out of herself—an' I'm free to say she did look better-natured, and no mistake—kind o' like a chokecherry in blossom, ye might say."

"An' then there's the Widder Glaspell," continued Perry, after a pause. "'Of course, anyone would expect she'd feel bad, seeing as how good David was to her boy—teaching him to play, ye know. But Mis' Glaspell says Joe jest does take on something terrible, and he won't tech the fiddle, though he was plum carried away with it when David was well and teaching of him. And there's the Clark kid. He's lame, ye know, and he thought the world and all of David's playing.

"'Course, there's you and Miss Holbrook, always asking and sending things—but that ain't so strange, 'cause you was 'specially his friends. But it's them others what beats me. Why, some days it's 'most every soul I meet, jest asking how he is, and saying they hopes he'll git well. Sometimes it's kids that he's played to, and I'll be triggered if one of 'em one day didn't have no excuse to

offer except that David had fit him—'bout a cat, or something—
and that ever since then he'd thought a heap of him—though he
guessed David didn't know it. Listen to that, will ye!

"An' once a woman held me up, and took on terrible, but all I
could git from her was that he'd sat on her doorstep and played
to her baby once or twice—as if that was anything! But one of the
funny ones was the woman who said she could wash her dishes
a sight easier after she'd a-seen him go by playing. There was Bill
Dowd, too. You know he really *has* got a screw loose in his head
somewheres, and there ain't anyone but what says he's the town
fool, all right. Well, what do ye think *he* said?"

Mr. Jack shook his head.

"Well, he said he did hope as how nothing would happen to
that boy because he did so like to see him smile, and that he always
did smile every time he met him! There, what do ye think o' that?"

"Well, I think, Perry," returned Mr. Jack soberly, "that Bill Dowd
wasn't playing the fool when he said that, quite so much as he
sometimes is, perhaps."

"Hmm, maybe not," murmured Perry Larson perplexedly. "Still,
I'm free to say I do think it was kind o' strange." He paused, then
slapped his knee suddenly. "Say, did I tell ye about Streeter—Old
Bill Streeter and the pear tree?"

Again Mr. Jack shook his head.

"Well, then, I'm going' to," declared the other, with gleeful
emphasis. "An', say, I don't believe even *you* can explain this, I
don't! Well, you know Streeter—every one does, so I ain't saying
nothing sland'rous. He was cut on a bias, and that bias runs to
money every time. You know as well as I do that he won't lift his
finger unless there's a dollar sticking to it, and that he hain't no use
for anything nor anybody unless there's money in it for him. I'm
blamed if I don't think that if he ever gets to heaven, he'll pluck his
own wings and sell the feathers for what they'll bring."

"Oh, Perry!" remonstrated Mr. Jack, in a half-stifled voice.

Perry Larson only grinned and went on imperturbably.

"Well, seeing as we both understand what he is, I'll tell ye what he done. He called me up to his fence one day, big as life, and says he, 'How's the boy?' and you could 'a' knocked me down with a feather. Streeter—a-asking how a boy was that was sick! and he seemed to care, too. I ain't seen him look so long-faced since— since he was paid up on a starting note I knows of, jest as he was smacking his lips over a nice fat farm that was coming to him!

"Well, I was that plum puzzled that I meant to find out why Streeter was taking such notice, if I hung for it. So I set to on a little detective work of my own, knowing, of course, that 't wasn't no use asking of him himself. Well, and what do you suppose I found out? If that little scamp of a boy hadn't even got round him—Streeter, the skinflint! He had—an' he went there often, the neighbors said; and Streeter doted on him. They declared that actually he give him a cent once—though that part I ain't swallering yet.

"They said—the neighbors did—that it all started from the pear tree—that big one to the left of his house. Maybe you remember it. Well, anyhow, it seems that it's old and through bearing any fruit, though it still blossoms fit to kill, every year, only a little late 'most always, and the blossoms stay on longer'n common, as if they knew there wasn't nothing doing later. Well, old Streeter said it had got to come down. I reckon he suspected it of swiping some of the sunshine, or maybe a little rain that belonged to the tree t'other side of the road what did bear fruit and was worth something! Anyhow, he got his man and his axe, and was plum ready to start in when he sees David and David sees him.

"It was when the boy first come. He'd gone to walk and had struck this pear tree, all in bloom—an' 'course, you know how the boy would act—a pear tree bloomin' is a likely sight, I'll own. He

danced and laughed and clapped his hands—he didn't have his
fiddle with him—an' carried on like all possessed. Then he sees the
man with the axe, and Streeter sees him.

"They said it was rich then—Bill Warner heard it all from
t'other side of the fence. He said that David, when he found out
what was going to happen, went clean crazy, and rampaged on
at such a rate that old Streeter couldn't do nothing but stand and
stare, until he finally managed to growl out: 'But I tell ye, boy, the
tree ain't no use no more!'

"Bill says the boy flew all to pieces then. 'No use—no use!' he
cries; 'such a perfectly beautiful thing as that no use! Why, it don't
have to be any use when it's so pretty. It's jest to look at and love,
and be happy with!' Fancy saying that to old Streeter! I'd like to
seen his face. But Bill says that wasn't half what the boy said. He
declared that it was God's present, anyhow, that trees was; and that
the things He give us to look at was jest as much use as the things
He give us to eat; and that the stars and the sunsets and the snowflakes and the little white cloud-boats, and I don't know what-all,
was jest as important in the Orchestra of Life as turnips and
squashes. And then, Billy says, he ended by jest flinging himself on
to Streeter and begging him to wait till he could go back and git
his fiddle so he could tell him what a beautiful thing that tree was.

"Well, if you'll believe it, old Streeter was so plum befuzzled he
sent the man and the axe away—an' that tree's a-livin' today—it
is!" he finished. Then, with a sudden gloom on his face, Larson
added, huskily: "An' I only hope I'll be saying the same thing of
that boy—come next month at this time!"

"We'll hope you will," sighed the other fervently.

And so one by one the days passed while the whole town
waited, and while in the great airy "parlor bedroom" of the Holly
farmhouse one small boy fought his battle for life. Then came the
blackest day and night of all when the town could only wait and

watch—it had lost its hope; when the doctors shook their heads and refused to meet Mrs. Holly's eyes; when the pulse in the slim wrist outside the coverlet played hide-and-seek with the cool, persistent fingers that sought so earnestly for it; when Perry Larson sat for uncounted sleepless hours by the kitchen stove and fearfully listened for a step crossing the hallway; when Mr. Jack on his porch, and Miss Holbrook in her tower window, went with David down into the dark valley, and came so near the rushing river that life, with its petty prides and prejudices, could never seem quite the same to them again.

Then, after that blackest day and night, came the dawn—as the dawns do come after the blackest of days and nights. In the slender wrist outside the coverlet the pulse gained and steadied. On the forehead beneath the nurse's fingers, a moisture came. The doctors nodded their heads now, and looked every one straight in the eye. "He will live," they said. "The crisis is passed." Out by the kitchen stove, Perry Larson heard the step cross the hall and sprang upright, but at the first glimpse of Mrs. Holly's tear-wet, yet radiant face, he collapsed limply.

"Say, do you know, I didn't suppose I did care so much! I reckon I'll go and tell Mr. Jack. He'll want to hear," he muttered.

CHAPTER 23

Puzzles

D AVID'S CONVALESCENCE WAS PICTURESQUE, IN A WAY. As soon as he was able, like a king he sat upon his throne and received his subjects; and a very gracious king he was, indeed. His room overflowed with flowers and fruit, and his bed quite groaned with the toys and books and games brought for his diversion, each one of which he hailed with delight, from Miss Holbrook's sumptuously bound Waverley Novels to little crippled Jimmy Clark's bag of marbles.

Only two things puzzled David: one was why everybody was so good to him, and the other was why he never could have the pleasure of both Mr. Jack's and Miss Holbrook's company at the same time.

David discovered this last curious circumstance concerning Mr. Jack and Miss Holbrook very early in his convalescence. It was on the second afternoon that Mr. Jack had been admitted to the sick-room. David had been hearing all the latest news of Jill and Joe, when suddenly he noticed an odd change come to his visitor's face.

The windows of the Holly "parlor bedroom" commanded a fine view of the road, and it was toward one of these windows that Mr. Jack's eyes were directed. David, sitting up in bed, saw then that down the road was approaching very swiftly a handsome span of black horses and an open carriage, which he had come to recognize as belonging to Miss Holbrook. He watched it eagerly now till he saw the horses turn in at the Holly driveway. Then he gave a low cry of delight.

"It's my Lady of the Roses! She's coming to see me. Look! Oh, I'm so glad! Now you'll see her, and just *know* how lovely she is. Why, Mr. Jack, you aren't going *now*!" he broke off in manifest disappointment as Mr. Jack leaped to his feet.

"I think I'll have to, if you don't mind, David," returned the man, an oddly nervous haste in his manner. "And you *won't* mind, now that you'll have Miss Holbrook. I want to speak to Larson. I saw him in the field out there a minute ago. And I guess I'll slip right through this window here, too, David. I don't want to lose him; and I can catch him quicker this way than any other," he finished, throwing up the sash.

"Oh, but Mr. Jack, please just wait a minute," begged David. "I wanted you to see my Lady of the Roses, and—" But Mr. Jack was already on the ground outside the low window; and the next minute, with a merry nod and smile, he had pulled the sash down after him and was hurrying away.

Almost at once, then, Miss Holbrook appeared at the bedroom door. "Mrs. Holly said I was to walk right in, David, so here I am," she began, in a cheery voice. "Oh, you're looking lots better than when I saw you Monday, young man!"

"I am better," caroled David. "And today I'm 'specially better, because Mr. Jack has been here."

"Oh, has Mr. Jack been to see you today?" There was an indefinable change in Miss Holbrook's voice.

"Yes, right now. Why, he was here when you were driving into the yard."

Miss Holbrook gave a perceptible start and looked about her a little wildly.

"Here when— But I didn't meet him anywhere in the hall."

"He didn't go through the hall," laughed David gleefully. "He went right through that window there."

"The window!" An angry flush mounted to Miss Holbrook's forehead. "Indeed, did he have to resort to that to escape—" She bit her lip and stopped abruptly.

David's eyes widened a little.

"Escape? Oh, *he* wasn't the one that was escaping. It was Perry. Mr. Jack was afraid he'd lose him. He saw him out the window there, right after he'd seen you, and he said he wanted to speak to him and he was afraid he'd get away. So he jumped right through that window there. See?"

"Oh, yes, I see," murmured Miss Holbrook, in a voice David thought was a little strange.

"I wanted him to stay," frowned David uncertainly. "I wanted him to see you."

"Dear me, David, I hope you didn't tell him so."

"Oh, yes, I did. But he couldn't stay, even then. You see, he wanted to catch Perry Larson."

"I've no doubt of it," retorted Miss Holbrook, with so much emphasis that David again looked at her with a slightly disturbed frown.

"But he'll come again soon, I'm sure, and then maybe you'll be here, too. I do so want him to see you, Lady of the Roses!"

"Nonsense, David!" laughed Miss Holbrook a little nervously. "Mr.—Mr. Gurnsey doesn't want to see me. He's seen me dozens of times."

"Oh, yes, he told me he'd seen you long ago," nodded David gravely, "but he didn't act as if he remembered it much."

"Didn't he, indeed!" laughed Miss Holbrook, again flushing a little. "Well, I'm sure, dear, we wouldn't want to tax the poor gentleman's memory too much, you know. Come, suppose you see what I've brought you," she finished gaily.

"Oh, what is it?" cried David as, under Miss Holbrook's swift fingers, the wrappings fell away and disclosed a box which, upon being opened, was found to be filled with quantities of oddly shaped bits of pictured wood—a jumble of confusion.

"It's a jigsaw puzzle, David. All these little pieces fit together to make a picture, you see. I tried last night and I couldn't do it. I brought it down to see if you could."

"Oh, thank you! I'd love to," rejoiced the boy. And in the fascination of the marvel of finding one fantastic bit that fitted another, David apparently forgot all about Mr. Jack—which seemed not unpleasing to his Lady of the Roses.

It was not until nearly a week later that David had his wish of seeing his Mr. Jack and his Lady of the Roses meet at his bedside. It was the day Miss Holbrook brought to him the wonderful set of handsomely bound Waverley Novels. He was still glorying in his new possession, in fact, when Mr. Jack appeared suddenly in the doorway.

"Hello, my boy, I just—Oh, I beg your pardon. I supposed you were—alone," he stammered, looking very red indeed.

"He is—that is, he will be soon—except for you, Mr. Gurnsey," smiled Miss Holbrook, very brightly. She was already on her feet.

"No, no, I beg of you," stammered Mr. Jack, growing still more red. "Don't let me drive—that is, I mean, don't go, please. I didn't know. I had no warning— I didn't see— Your carriage was not at the door today."

Miss Holbrook's eyebrows rose the fraction of an inch. "I sent it home. I am planning to walk back. I have several calls to make on the way, and it's high time I was starting. Goodbye, David."

"But, Lady of the Roses, please, please, don't go," besought David, who had been looking from one to the other in worried dismay. "Why, you've just come!"

But neither coaxing nor argument availed, and before David

really knew just what had happened, he found himself alone with Mr. Jack.

Even then disappointment was piled on disappointment, for Mr. Jack's visit was not the unalloyed happiness it usually was. Mr. Jack himself was almost cross at first, and then he was silent and restless, moving jerkily about the room in a way that disturbed David very much.

Mr. Jack had brought with him a book, but even that only made matters worse, for when he saw the beautifully bound volumes that Miss Holbrook had just left, he frowned and told David that he guessed he did not need his gift at all, with all those other fine books. And David could not seem to make him understand that the one book from him was just exactly as dear as were the whole set of books that his Lady of the Roses brought.

Certainly it was not a satisfactory visit at all; and for the first time, David was almost glad to have Mr. Jack go and leave him with his books. The books, David told himself, he could understand; Mr. Jack he could not—not today.

Several times after this, David's Lady of the Roses and Mr. Jack happened to call at the same hour; but never could David persuade these two friends of his to stay together. Always, if one came and the other was there, the other went away, in spite of David's protestations that two people did not tire him at all and his assertions that he often entertained as many as that at once. Tractable as they were in all other ways, anxious as they seemed to please him, on this one point they were obdurate: never would they stay together.

They were not angry with each other—David was sure of that, for they were always very especially polite, and rose, and stood, and bowed in a most delightful fashion. Still, he sometimes thought that they did not quite like each other, for always, after the one went away, the other, left behind, was silent and almost stern—if it was Mr. Jack—and flushed-faced and nervous if it was Miss Holbrook. But why this was so, David could not understand.

The span of handsome black horses came very frequently to the Holly farmhouse now, and as time passed, they often bore away behind them a white-faced but happy-eyed boy on the seat beside Miss Holbrook.

"My, but I don't see how everyone can be so good to me!" exclaimed the boy one day to his Lady of the Roses.

"Oh, that's easy, David," she smiled. "The only trouble is to find out what you want—you ask for so little."

"But I don't need to ask—you do it all beforehand," asserted the boy, "you and Mr. Jack, and everybody."

"Really? That's good." For a brief moment, Miss Holbrook hesitated. Then, as if casually, she asked, "And he tells you stories, too, I suppose—this Mr. Jack—just as he used to, doesn't he?"

"Well, he never did tell me but one, you know, before; but he's told me more now, since I've been sick."

"Oh, yes, I remember, and that one was 'The Princess and the Pauper,' wasn't it? Well, has he told you any more—like—that?"

The boy shook his head with decision.

"No, he doesn't tell me any more like that, and—and I don't want him to, either."

Miss Holbrook laughed a little oddly. "Why, David, what is the matter with that?" she queried.

"The ending; it wasn't nice, you know."

"Oh, yes, I—I remember."

"I've asked him to change it," David went on, in a grieved voice. "I asked him just the other day, but he wouldn't."

"Perhaps he—he didn't want to." Miss Holbrook spoke very quickly, but so low that David barely heard the words.

"Didn't want to? Oh, yes, he did! He looked awful sober, and as if he really cared, you know. And he said he'd give all he had in the world if he really could change it, but he couldn't."

"Did he say—just that?" Miss Holbrook was leaning forward a little breathlessly now.

"Yes, just that. And that's the part I couldn't understand," commented David. "For I don't see why a story—just a story made up out of somebody's head—can't be changed any way you want it. And I told him so."

"Well, and what did he say to that?"

"He didn't say anything for a minute, and I had to ask him again. Then he sat up suddenly, just as if he'd been asleep, you know, and said, 'Eh, what, David?' And then I told him again what I'd said. This time he shook his head and smiled that kind of a smile that isn't really a smile, you know, and said something about a real, true-to-life story's never having but one ending, and that was a logical ending. Lady of the Roses, what is a logical ending?"

The Lady of the Roses laughed unexpectedly. The two little red spots that David always loved to see flamed into her cheeks, and her eyes showed a sudden sparkle. When she answered, her words came disconnectedly, with little laughing breaths between.

"Well, David, I—I'm not sure I can tell you. But perhaps I can find out. This much, however, I am sure of: Mr. Jack's logical ending wouldn't be mine!"

What she meant David did not know, nor would she tell him when he asked, but a few days later she sent for him, and David— able now to go where he pleased—very gladly obeyed the summons.

It was November, and the garden was bleak and cold; but in the library a bright fire danced on the hearth, and before this Miss Holbrook drew up two low chairs.

She looked particularly pretty, David thought. The rich red of her dress had apparently brought out an answering red in her cheeks. Her eyes were very bright and her lips smiled, yet she seemed oddly nervous and restless. She sewed a little, with a bit of yellow silk on white—but not for long. She knitted with two long ivory needles flashing in and out of a silky mesh of blue—but this, too, she soon ceased doing. On a low stand at David's side she had placed books and pictures, and for a time she talked of those. Then very abruptly she asked, "David, when will you see—Mr. Jack again—do you suppose?"

"Tomorrow. I'm going up to the House that Jack Built to tea, and I'm to stay all night. Mr. Jack is going to show me what a fall party is like. He's planned lots of things for Jill and me to do, with nuts and apples and candles, you know. It's tomorrow night, so I'll see him then."

"Tomorrow? So—so soon?" faltered Miss Holbrook. And to David, gazing at her with wondering eyes, it almost seemed for a moment as if she were looking about for a place to which she might run and hide. Then determinedly, as if she were taking hold of something with both hands, she leaned forward, looked David squarely in the eyes, and began to talk hurriedly, yet very distinctly.

"David, listen. I've something I want you to say to Mr. Jack, and I want you to be sure and get it just right. It's about the—the story, 'The Princess and the Pauper,' you know. You can remember, I think, for you remembered that so well. Will you say it to him— what I'm going to tell you—just as I say it?"

"Why, of course, I will!" David's promise was unhesitating, though his eyes were still puzzled.

"It's about the—the ending," stammered Miss Holbrook. "That is, it may—it may have something to do with the ending— perhaps," she finished lamely. And again David noticed that odd shifting of Miss Holbrook's gaze as if she was searching for some means of escape. Then, as before, he saw her chin lift determinedly as she began to talk faster than ever.

"Now, listen," she admonished him, earnestly.

And David listened.

CHAPTER 24

A Story Remodeled

THE FALL PARTY WAS A GREAT SUCCESS. So VERY EXCITED, indeed, did David become over the swinging apples and popping nuts that he quite forgot to tell Mr. Jack what the Lady of the Roses had said until Jill had gone up to bed and he himself was about to take the little lighted lamp from Mr. Jack's hand.

"Oh, Mr. Jack, I forgot," he cried then. "There was something I was going to tell you."

"Never mind tonight, David; it's so late. Suppose we leave it until tomorrow," suggested Mr. Jack, still with the lamp extended in his hand.

"But I promised the Lady of the Roses that I'd say it tonight," demurred the boy, in a troubled voice.

The man drew his lamp halfway back suddenly. "The Lady of the Roses! Do you mean—she sent a message—to *me*?" he demanded.

"Yes, about the story 'The Princess and the Pauper,' you know."

With an abrupt exclamation, Mr. Jack set the lamp on the table and turned to a chair. He had apparently lost his haste to go to bed.

"See here, David, suppose you come and sit down, and tell me just what you're talking about. And first, just what does the Lady of the Roses know about that—that 'Princess and the Pauper'?"

"Why, she knows it all, of course," returned the boy in surprise. "I told it to her."

"You—told—it—to her!" Mr. Jack relaxed in his chair. "David!"

"Yes. And she was just as interested as could be."

"I don't doubt it!" Mr. Jack's lips snapped together a little grimly.

"Only she didn't like the ending, either."

Mr. Jack sat up suddenly. "She didn't like—David, are you sure? Did she *say* that?"

David frowned in thought.

"Well, I don't know as I can tell, exactly, but I'm sure she didn't like it, because just before she told me *what* to say to you, she said that—that what she was going to say would probably have something to do with the ending, anyway. Still—" David paused in yet deeper thought. "Come to think of it, there really isn't anything—not in what she said—that *changed* that ending, as I can see. They didn't get married and live happy ever after, anyhow."

"Yes, but what did she say?" asked Mr. Jack in a voice that was not quite steady. "Now, be careful, David, and tell it just as she said it."

"Oh, I will," nodded David. "She said to do that, too."

"Did she?" Mr. Jack leaned farther forward in his chair. "But tell me, how did she happen to—to say anything about it? Suppose you begin at the beginning—away back, David. I want to hear it all—all!"

David gave a contented sigh, and settled himself more comfortably.

"Well, to begin with, you see, I told her the story long ago, before I was sick, and she was ever so interested then, and asked lots of questions. Then the other day something came up—I've forgotten how—about the ending, and I told her how hard I'd tried to have you change it, but you wouldn't. And she spoke right up quick and said probably you didn't want to change it, anyhow. But, of course, I settled *that* question without any trouble," went on David confidently, "by just telling her how you said you'd give anything in the world to change it."

"And you told her that—just that, David?" cried the man.

"Why, yes, I had to," answered David, in surprise, "else she wouldn't have known that you *did* want to change it. Don't you see?"

"Oh, yes! I—see—a good deal that I'm thinking you don't," muttered Mr. Jack, falling back in his chair.

"Well, then is when I told her about the logical ending—what you said, you know. Oh, yes! And that was when I found out she didn't like the ending, because she laughed such a funny little laugh and colored up, and said that she wasn't sure she could tell me what a logical ending was, but that she would try to find out, and that, anyhow, *your* ending wouldn't be hers—she was sure of that."

"David, did she say that—really?" Mr. Jack was on his feet now.

"She did. And then yesterday she asked me to come over, and she said some more things—about the story, I mean—but she didn't say another thing about the ending. She didn't ever say anything about that except that little bit I told you of a minute ago."

"Yes, yes, but what did she say?" demanded Mr. Jack, stopping short in his walk up and down the room.

"She said: 'You tell Mr. Jack that *I* know something about that story of his that perhaps he doesn't. In the first place, I know the Princess a lot better than he does, and she isn't a bit the kind of girl he's pictured her.'"

"Yes! Go on—go on!"

"'Now, for instance,' she says, 'when the boy made that call after the girl first came back, and when the boy didn't like it because they talked of colleges and travels, and such things, you tell him that I happen to know that that girl was just hoping and hoping he'd speak of the old days and games; but that *she* couldn't speak, of course, when he hadn't been even once to see her during all those weeks, and when he'd acted in every way just as if he'd forgotten.'"

"But she hadn't waved—that Princess hadn't waved—once!" argued Mr. Jack; "and he looked and looked for it."

"Yes, *she* spoke of that," returned David. "But *she* said she shouldn't think the Princess would have waved, when she'd got to be such a great big girl as that—*waving to a boy*! She said that, for her part, she should have been ashamed of her if she had!"

"Oh, did she!" murmured Mr. Jack blankly, dropping suddenly into his chair.

"Yes, she did," repeated David, with a little virtuous uplifting of his chin.

It was plain to be seen that David's sympathies had unaccountably met with a change of heart.

"But—the Pauper—"

"Oh, yes, and that's another thing," interrupted David. "The Lady of the Roses said that she didn't like that name one bit; that it wasn't true, anyway, because he wasn't a pauper. And she said, too, that as for his picturing the princess as being perfectly happy in all that magnificence, he didn't get it right at all. For *she* knew that the Princess wasn't one bit happy because she was so lonesome for things and people she had known when she was just the girl."

Again Mr. Jack sprang to his feet. For a minute he strode up and down the room in silence; then in a shaking voice he asked, "David, you—you aren't making all this up, are you? You're saying just what—what Miss Holbrook told you to?"

"Why, of course, I'm not making it up," protested the boy aggrievedly. "This is the Lady of the Roses' story—*she* made it up—only she talked it as if it was real, of course, just as you did. She said another thing, too. She said that she happened to know that the princess had got all that magnificence around her in the first place just to see if it wouldn't make her happy, but that it hadn't, and that now she had one place—a little room—that was left just as it used to be when she was the girl, and that she went there and sat very often. And she said it was right in sight of where the boy lived, too, where he could see it every day, and that if he hadn't been so blind, he could have looked right through those gray walls and seen that, and seen lots of other things. And what did she mean by that, Mr. Jack?"

"I don't know—I don't know, David," half-groaned Mr. Jack. "Sometimes I think she means—and then I think that can't be—true."

"But do you think it's helped it any—the story?" persisted the boy. "She's only talked a little about the princess. She didn't really change things any—not the ending."

"But she said it might, David—she said it might! Don't you remember?" cried the man eagerly. And to David, his eagerness did not seem at all strange. Mr. Jack had said before—long ago—that he would be very glad indeed to have a happier ending to this tale. "Think now," continued the man. "Perhaps she said something else, too. Did she say anything else, David?"

David shook his head slowly.

"No, only—yes, there was a little something, but it doesn't *change* things any, for it was only a 'supposing.' She said: 'Just supposing, after long years, that the Princess found out about how the boy felt long ago, and suppose he should look up at the tower someday, at the old time, and see a *one—two* wave, which meant, "Come over to see me." Just what do you suppose he would do?' But of course, *that* can't do any good," finished David gloomily as he rose to go to bed, "for that was only a 'supposing.'"

"Of course," agreed Mr. Jack steadily; and David did not know that only stern self-control had forced the steadiness into that voice, nor that, for Mr. Jack, the whole world had burst suddenly into song.

Neither did David, the next morning, know that long before eight o'clock, Mr. Jack stood at a certain window, his eyes unswervingly fixed on the gray towers of Sunnycrest. What David did know, however, was that just after eight, Mr. Jack strode through the room where he and Jill were playing checkers, flung himself into his hat and coat, and then fairly leaped down the steps toward the path that led to the footbridge at the bottom of the hill.

"Why, whatever in the world ails Jack?" gasped Jill. Then, after a startled pause, she asked. "David, do folks ever go crazy for joy? Yesterday, you see, Jack got two splendid pieces of news. One was from his doctor. He was examined, and he's fine, the doctor says; all well, so he can go back now, any time, to the city and work. I shall go to school then, you know—a young ladies' school," she finished, a little importantly.

"He's well? How splendid! But what was the other news? You said there were two; only it couldn't have been nicer than that was; to be well—all well!"

"The other? Well, that was only that his old place in the city was waiting for him. He was with a firm of big lawyers, you know. And, of course, it is nice to have a place all waiting. But I can't see anything in those things to make him act like this now. Can you?"

"Why, yes, maybe," declared David. "He's found his work— don't you see?—out in the world, and he's going to do it. I know how I'd feel if I had found mine that Father told me of! Only what I can't understand is, if Mr. Jack knew all this yesterday, why didn't he act like this then, instead of waiting till today?"

"I wonder," said Jill.

CHAPTER 25

The Beautiful World

DAVID FOUND MANY NEW SONGS IN HIS VIOLIN THOSE early winter days, and they were very beautiful ones. To begin with, there were all the kindly looks and deeds that were showered upon him from every side. There was the first snowstorm, too, with the feathery flakes turning all the world to fantastic whiteness. This song David played to Mr. Streeter one day, and great was his disappointment that the man could not seem to understand what the song said.

"But don't you see?" pleaded David. "I'm telling you that it's your pear tree blossoms come back to say how glad they are that you didn't kill them that day."

"Pear tree blossoms—come back!" ejaculated the old man. "Well, no, I can't see. Where's yer pear tree blossoms?"

"Why, there—out of the window—everywhere," urged the boy.

"There! By ginger! Boy—ye don't mean—ye can't mean the *snow*!"

"Of course, I do! Now can't you see it? Why, the whole tree was just a great big cloud of snowflakes. Don't you remember? Well, now it's gone away and got a whole lot more trees, and all the little white petals have come dancing down to celebrate, and to tell you they sure are coming back next year."

"Well, by ginger!" exclaimed the man again. Then, suddenly, he threw back his head with a hearty laugh. David did not quite like the laugh; neither did he care for the five-cent piece that the man thrust into his fingers a little later, though—had David but known it—both the laugh and the five-cent piece gift were—for the uncomprehending man who gave them—white milestones along an unfamiliar way.

It was soon after this that there came to David the great surprise—his beloved Lady of the Roses and his no less beloved Mr. Jack were to be married at the beginning of the New Year. So very surprised, indeed, was David at this that even his violin was mute and had nothing, at first, to say about it. But to Mr. Jack, as man to man, David said one day, "I thought men, when they married women, went courting. In storybooks they do. And you— you hardly ever said a word to my beautiful Lady of the Roses. And you spoke once—long ago—as if you scarcely remembered her at all. Now, what do you mean by that?"

And Mr. Jack laughed, but he grew red, too—and then he told it all—that it was just the story of "The Princess and the Pauper," and that he, David, had been the one, as it happened, to do part of their courting for them.

And how David had laughed then, and how he had fairly hugged himself for joy! And when next he had picked up his violin, what a beautiful, beautiful song he had found about it in the vibrant strings!

It was this same song, as it chanced, that he was playing in his room that Saturday afternoon when the letter from Simeon Holly's long-lost son John came to the Holly farmhouse.

Downstairs in the kitchen, Simeon Holly stood with the letter in his hand. "Ellen, we've got a letter from—John," he said. That Simeon Holly spoke of it at all showed how very far along his unfamiliar way he had come since the last letter from John had arrived.

"From—John? Oh, Simeon! From John?"

"Yes."

Simeon sat down and tried to hide the shaking of his hand as he ran the point of his knife under the flap of the envelope. "We'll see what he says." And to hear him, one might have thought that letters from John were everyday occurrences.

DEAR FATHER: Twice before I have written [ran the letter], and received no answer. But I'm going to make one more effort for forgiveness. May I not come to you this Christmas? I have a little boy of my own now, and my heart aches for you. I know how I should feel, should he, in years to come, do as I did.

I'll not deceive you—I have not given up my art. You told me once to choose between you and it—and I chose, I suppose; at least, I ran away. Yet in the face of all that, I ask you again, may I not come to you at Christmas? I want you, Father, and I want Mother. And I want you to see my boy.

"Well?" said Simeon Holly, trying to speak with a steady coldness that would not show how deeply moved he was. "Well, Ellen?"

"Yes, Simeon, yes!" choked his wife, a world of mother-love and longing in her pleading eyes and voice. "Yes—you'll let it be—'Yes'!"

"Uncle Simeon, Aunt Ellen," called David, clattering down the stairs from his room, "I've found such a beautiful song in my violin, and I'm going to play it over and over so as to be sure and remember it for Father—for it is a beautiful world, Uncle Simeon, isn't it? Now, listen!"

And Simeon Holly listened, but it was not the violin that he heard. It was the voice of a little curly-headed boy out of the past.

When David stopped playing some time later, only the woman sat watching him—the man was over at his desk, pen in hand.

John, John's wife, and John's boy came the day before Christmas, and great was the excitement in the Holly farmhouse. John was found to be big, strong, and bronzed with the outdoor life of many a sketching trip—a son to be proud of and to be leaned upon in one's old age. Mrs. John, according to Perry Larson, was "the slickest little woman going." According to John's mother, she was an almost unbelievable fruition of a long-dreamed-of, long-despaired-of daughter—sweet, lovable, and charmingly beautiful. Little John—little John was himself; and he could not have been more had he been an angel-cherub straight from heaven—which, in fact, he was, in his doting grandparents' eyes.

John Holly had been at his old home less than four hours when he chanced upon David's violin. He was with his father and mother at the time. There was no one else in the room. With a sidelong glance at his parents, he picked up the instrument—John Holly had not forgotten his own youth. His violin-playing in the old days had not been welcome, he remembered.

"A fiddle! Who plays?" he asked.

"David."

"Oh, the boy. You say you took him in? By the way, what an odd little shaver he is! Never did I see a boy like him."

Simeon Holly's head came up almost aggressively. "David is a good boy—a very good boy, indeed, John. We think a great deal of him."

John Holly laughed lightly, yet his brow carried a puzzled frown. Two things John Holly had not been able thus far to understand: an indefinable change in his father, and the position of the boy, David, in the household. John Holly was still remembering his own repressed youth.

"Hmm," he murmured, softly picking the strings, then drawing a tentative bow across them. "I've a fiddle at home that I play sometimes. Do you mind if I—tune her up?"

A flicker of something that was very near to humor flashed from his father's eyes. "Oh, no. We are used to that—now."

And again John Holly remembered his youth. "Oh, but he's got the dandy instrument here," cried the player, dropping his bow after the first half-dozen superbly vibrant tones, and carrying the violin to the window. A moment later he gave an amazed cry and turned a dumbfounded face toward his father.

"Great Scott, Father! Where did that boy get this instrument? I know something of violins, if I can't play them much; and this—! Where did he get it?"

"Of his father, I suppose. He had it when he came here, anyway."

"'Had it when he came'! But, Father, you said he was a tramp, and—oh, come, tell me, what is the secret behind this? Here I come home and find calmly reposing on my father's sitting-room table a violin that's priceless, for all I know. Anyhow, I do know that its value is reckoned in the thousands, not hundreds. And yet you, with equal calmness, tell me it's owned by this boy who, it's safe to say, doesn't know how to play sixteen notes on it correctly, to say nothing of appreciating those he does play; and who, by your own account, is nothing but—" A swiftly uplifted hand of warning stayed the words on his lips. He turned to see David himself in the doorway.

"Come in, David," said Simeon Holly quietly. "My son wants to hear you play. I don't think he has heard you." And again there flashed from Simeon Holly's eyes a something very much like humor.

With obvious hesitation, John Holly relinquished the violin. From the expression on his face it was plain to be seen the sort of torture he deemed was before him. But, as if constrained to ask the question, he did say, "Where did you get this violin, boy?"

"I don't know. We've always had it, ever since I could remember—this and the other one."

"The *other* one!"

"Father's."

"Oh!" He hesitated; then, a little severely, he observed, "This is a fine instrument, boy—a very fine instrument."

"Yes," nodded David, with a cheerful smile. "Father said it was. I like it, too. This is an Amati, but the other is a Stradivarius. Sometimes I don't know which I do like best; only *this* is mine."

With a half-smothered exclamation, John Holly fell back limply. "Then you—do—know?" he challenged.

"Know—what?"

"The value of that violin in your hands."

There was no answer. The boy's eyes were questioning.

"The worth, I mean—what it's worth."

"Why, no—yes—that is, it's worth everything to me," answered David, in a puzzled voice.

With an impatient gesture, John Holly brushed this aside. "But the other one—where is that?"

"At Joe Glaspell's. I gave it to him to play on, because he hadn't any, and he liked to play so well."

"You *gave* it to him—a Stradivarius!"

"I loaned it to him," corrected David, in a troubled voice. "Being Father's, I couldn't bear to give it away. But Joe—Joe had to have something to play on."

"'Something to play on'! Father, he doesn't mean the River Street Glaspells?" cried John Holly.

"I think he does. Joe is old Peleg Glaspell's grandson." John Holly threw up both his hands.

"A Stradivarius—to old Peleg's grandson! Oh!" he muttered. "Well, I'll be—" He did not finish his sentence, for at another word from Simeon Holly, David had begun to play.

From his seat by the stove, Simeon Holly watched his son's face—and smiled. He saw amazement, unbelief, and delight struggle for the mastery; but before the playing had ceased, he was summoned by Perry Larson to the kitchen on a matter of business. So it was into the kitchen that John Holly burst a little later, eyes and cheek aflame.

"Father, where in the world *did* you get that boy?" he demanded. "Who taught him to play like that? I've been trying to find out from him, but I'd defy Sherlock Holmes himself to make head or tail of the sort of lingo he talks, about mountain homes and the Orchestra of Life! Father, what does it mean?"

Obediently, Simeon Holly told the story then, more fully than he had told it before. He brought forward the letter, too, with its mysterious signature.

"Perhaps you can make it out, Son," he laughed. "None of the rest of us can, though I haven't shown it to anybody now for a long time. I got discouraged long ago of anybody's ever making it out."

"Make it out—make it out!" cried John Holly excitedly. "I should say I could! It's a name known the world over. It's the name of one of the greatest violinists that ever lived."

"But how—what—how came he in my barn?" demanded Simeon Holly.

"Easily guessed from the letter, and from what the world knows," returned John, his voice still shaking with excitement. "He was always a strange chap, they say, and full of his notions. Six or eight years ago his wife died. They say he utterly adored her, and for weeks refused even to touch his violin. Then, very suddenly, he, with his four-year-old son, disappeared—dropped quite out of sight. Some people guessed the reason. I knew a man who was well acquainted with him, and at the time of the disappearance, he told me quite a lot about him. He said he wasn't a bit surprised at what had happened, that already half a dozen relatives were interfering with the way he wanted to bring the boy up, and that David was in a fair way to be spoiled, even then, with so much attention and flattery. The father had determined to make a wonderful artist of his son, and he was known to have said that he believed—as do so many others—that the first dozen years of a child's life are the making of the man, and that if he could have the boy to himself that long, he would risk the rest. So it seems he carried out his notion until he was taken sick and had to quit—poor chap!"

"But why didn't he tell us plainly in that note who he was, then?" fumed Simeon Holly, in manifest irritation.

"He did, he thought," laughed the other. "He signed his name, and he supposed that was so well known that just to mention it would be enough. That's why he kept it so secret while he was living on the mountain, you see, and that's why even David himself didn't know it. Of course, if anybody found out who he was, that ended his scheme, and he knew it. So he supposed all he had to do at the last was to sign his name to that note, and everybody would know who he was, and David would at once be sent to his own people. (There's an aunt and some cousins, I believe.) You see he didn't reckon on nobody's being able to *read* his name! Besides, being so ill, he probably wasn't quite sane, anyway."

"I see, I see," nodded Simeon Holly, frowning a little. "And of course if we had made it out, some of us here would have known it, probably. Now that you call it to mind, I think I have heard it myself in days gone by—though such names mean little to me. But doubtless somebody would have known. However, that is all past and gone now."

"Oh, yes, and no harm done. He fell into good hands. You'll soon see the last of him now, of course."

"Last of him? Oh, no, I shall keep David," said Simeon Holly with decision.

"Keep him! Why, Father, you forget who he is! There are friends, relatives, an adoring public, and a mint of money awaiting that boy. You can't keep him. You could never have kept him this long if this little town of yours hadn't been buried in this forgotten valley up among these hills. You'll have the whole world at your doors the minute they find out he is here—hills or no hills! Besides, there are his people; they have some claim."

There was no answer. With a suddenly old, drawn look on his face, the elder man had turned away.

Half an hour later, Simeon Holly climbed the stairs to David's room, and as gently and plainly as he could told the boy of this great, good thing that had come to him.

David was amazed but overjoyed. That he was found to be the son of a famous man affected him not at all, only so far as it seemed to set his father right in other eyes—in David's own, the man had always been supreme. But the going away—the marvelous going away—filled him with excited wonder.

"You mean, I shall go away and study—practice—learn more of my violin?"

"Yes, David."

"And hear beautiful music like the organ in church, only more—bigger—better?"

"I suppose so."

"And know people—dear people—who will understand what I say when I play?"

Simeon Holly's face paled a little. Still, he knew David had not meant to make it so hard. "Yes."

"Why, it's my 'start'—just what I was going to have with the gold pieces," cried David joyously. Then, uttering a sharp cry of consternation, he clapped his fingers to his lips.

"Your—what?" asked the man.

"N—nothing, really, Mr. Holly—Uncle Simeon—n—nothing."

Something, either the boy's agitation, or the mention of the gold pieces sent a sudden dismayed suspicion into Simeon Holly's eyes. "Your 'start'?—the 'gold pieces'? David, what do you mean?"

David shook his head. He did not intend to tell. But gently, persistently, Simeon Holly questioned until the whole piteous little tale lay bare before him: the hopes, the house of dreams, the sacrifice.

David saw then what it means when a strong man is shaken by an emotion that has mastered him; and the sight awed and frightened the boy.

"Mr. Holly, is it because I'm—going—that you care—so much? I never thought—or supposed—you'd—*care*," he faltered.

There was no answer. Simeon Holly's eyes were turned quite away.

"Uncle Simeon—*please*! I—I think I don't want to go, anyway. I—I'm sure I don't want to go—and leave *you*!"

Simeon Holly turned then, and spoke. "Go? Of course you'll go, David. Do you think I'd tie you here to me—*now*?" he choked. "What don't I owe to you—home, son, happiness! Go?—of course you'll go. I wonder if you really think I'd let you stay! Come, we'll go down to Mother and tell her. I suspect she'll want to start in tonight to get your socks all mended up!" And with head erect and a determined step, Simeon Holly faced the mighty sacrifice in his turn, and led the way downstairs.

$$* \quad * \quad *$$

The friends, the relatives, the adoring public, the mint of money—they are all David's now. But once each year, man grown though he is, he picks up his violin and journeys to a little village far up among the hills. There in a quiet kitchen he plays to an old man and an old woman; and always to himself he says that he is practicing against the time when, his violin at his chin and the bow drawn across the strings, he shall go to meet his father in the far-away land, and tell him of the beautiful world he has left.

More Books from The Good and the Beautiful Library

Mystery on Heron Shoals Island
by Augusta Huiell Seaman

The Threatening Fog
by Leon Ware

The Dragon's Secret
by Augusta Huiell Seaman

Black Hawk
by Arthur J. Beckhard

goodandbeautiful.com